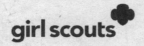
girl scouts

Maven Takes the Lead

Written by Yamile Saied Méndez

HARPER
An Imprint of HarperCollinsPublishers

Library of Congress Control Number: 2024940310
ISBN 978-0-06-331781-9
Art by Jennifer Bricking
Book design by Alison Klapthor

24 25 26 27 28   PC/CWR   10 9 8 7 6 5 4 3 2 1
First Edition

To all the friends, near and far—your kindness, care, and commitment make the world a better place.

—Girl Scouts

To Maven Rojas and Amparo Ortiz, for letting me name such an amazing character after them.

—Y.S.M.

Chapter One

The sun was sinking quickly under the horizon, and Maven got excited.

She'd timed their final adventure of the summer epically. In two minutes, her brother Gabriel and their cousins, the most adorable triplets ever, were going to get the show of their lives. It would be the perfect way to end Camp Maven.

But not if they kept looking at the bottom of Gabriel's shoe.

"Let's go, chickadees!" Maven called.

Her cheery voice didn't even pierce through the fascination over the smear on Gabriel's shoe though.

"Do you think it's a triceratops's or a brontosaurus's droppings, Grabiel?" Grey asked.

The way he pronounced Gabriel's name never failed to make Maven smile. He might be only four, but after the dinosaur adventure Maven had planned back in June, he was an expert in dinosaurs now.

"Hm, I'm not sure," Gabriel replied. "If it was a brontosaurus, we'd already have seen it by now."

"Really? You think so, Grabiel?"

With a mix of excitement and fear in his eyes, Grey looked over the lush canopies of the Forest of Magicstan as if he expected a pod of giant lizards to come out and surprise them.

"It's not dinosaur droppings, Grey," Ruby, one of his sisters, said. There was laughter in her voice, but still, she looked at the trees nervously.

Valentina, the other triplet, placed a calming hand over Grey's shoulder. She too must have seen the fear in his eyes. With a soft voice, she said, "I think this is where the cows run away sometimes. The dinosaurs are getting ready to hibernate since school's starting tomorrow."

"Dinosaurs don't hibernate, Val!" Grey complained, but his eyes crinkled with a smile.

Luckily, Lucho, their shaggy dog, came to the rescue.

He started barking and pulled them back to the adventure at hand.

"Come on!" Maven insisted. "Lucho wants to show us something fantastic!"

"Race you to Fairy Meadow!" Gabriel took off uphill. The rest of the little ones dashed after him.

Relieved, Maven glanced at her watch. Crisis averted.

She adjusted her backpack full of supplies and followed them just as the *fairy* show got started.

"Fairies are real!" Valentina squealed with delight, jumping up and down. The pink-and-yellow silk butterfly wings attached to her wrists waved in the light breeze.

"Shhh, Val!" Grey whispered, but he was jumping with excitement too. "You're going to scare them!"

Lucho circled around the kids, just as Maven had trained him for when she needed to round them up. They sat on the picnic blanket she'd already laid out and watched the blinking lights with pure wonder.

Maven passed out snacks—juice boxes and cheese and crackers—and knelt next to the kids to enjoy the fairies too. The loyal pup licked her face and sat by her side, but he was quivering. It was all he could do not to streak toward the blinking lights and catch one or two as his own snack. Thank goodness he was obedient.

She didn't want this outing to become a horror scene if their dog ate any of the *fairies.*

They weren't fairies, of course, just fireflies. But all summer long, Maven had taken her brother and their cousins, and occasionally Gabriel's friends, on adventures around their neighborhood. She'd written a field guide and created elaborate plans for themed activities: dinosaurs, pirates, mermaids, Olympics, rocks and minerals, until they reached the best one yet—fairies.

Every morning this week, they had talked about different kind of fairies (woodland, water, and fire), and she told them stories she wrote the night before. The stories weren't original but retellings of books she'd read before. The little kids loved it when she put her own spin on them. Their appetite for new material was never-ending.

Seeing a fairy in real life would be the highlight of their summer.

The cherry on top of their adventures.

The icing on the cake of their imagination.

Typical Maven, she'd been worried the clouds would turn to rain, or that the fireflies wouldn't come out, or that the triplets would be cranky. They never stayed up beyond 7:00 p.m., but their mom, Tía Janette, had given them special permission since it was the last weekend before school started on Monday. Tía Janette was Maven's aunt on her mom's side.

But, so far, everything was going according to plan. Maven's plan.

And then she'd finally have time to get ready for the upcoming months.

Tomorrow would be full of preparations for the new school year. Maven would be in fifth grade, which was strange to think about. In her school, fifth grade was the oldest grade. Last year though, the kids had seemed so much older and cooler than her. She'd grown half an inch this summer, but she still didn't feel older. Or cooler. She'd loved every moment she'd spent with the little ones, but maybe now she was too used to hanging out with them.

Hopefully things would change once school started and something would click and make her cool.

Suddenly, Gabriel pointed toward the middle of the meadow, and the triplets gasped.

"Look at that!" Gabriel exclaimed, trying to keep his voice down.

A cluster of pulsing lights hovered over the last of the season's wildflowers.

"That's definitely where the queen lives," Ruby whispered. "Right, Maven?"

Maven nodded. "Right! That's the capital of Magicstan."

"I love this place," Gabriel said, his wide smile showing the little window left when his two top teeth had fallen out a few days ago. He was seven, three years older than the triplets and three years younger than Maven. Sometimes he liked to pretend he was all grown up, but he was still very much a kid.

The view was so magical, even for him.

Emerald Hill, Fairy Meadow, and Fantastic Forest were really the undeveloped lots in their neighborhood, the Pleasant Meadows subdivision in the outskirts of Savannah, Georgia. Maven may have planned the outing, but Mother Nature had given her a hand. The mist from the nearby creek gave the scene the touch of magic Maven could only dream about.

"Unlike dinosaurs, fairies do hibernate," Maven said, reminding them of the lesson from yesterday morning. "Now, all of fairyland is dancing and celebrating the end of a successful season. They worked so hard all summer. It's time to rest now. They'll wake up in the spring to paint the flowers and the leaves in the brightest colors."

"But it's not officially fall for like one more month," Gabriel said, narrowing his eyes suspiciously.

He always complained that school started just as summer was reaching its peak in the middle of August. He had a good point.

"The fairies run on their own calendar, Gabe," Maven said. "Their ways are mysterious."

Gabriel seemed satisfied with her answer.

Valentina slapped at her own arm, and Maven already had the mosquito repellent at hand. She sprayed the kids so they wouldn't get bitten. The four of them looked so happy that she hoped to remember this for a long time.

Before the sun's glow in the horizon dimmed, she took out her camera and snapped pictures of all of them as they watched the fireflies blink and wink.

They too didn't want summer to be over yet.

A couple of hours later, Tía Janette walked home with the sleepy triplets. After his bath, Gabriel fell asleep on the couch with his sketch pad in hand. Papi carried him to bed. Maven headed to her room to write an account of the day in her journal.

It was shocking that the summer was gone.

When her parents had told her that this year they wouldn't be able to travel anywhere because of work schedules, Maven had been sad. But not for long.

She'd looked forward to spending it all with Gemma.

The girls had been in the same class and best friends since pre-pre-K and they had clicked immediately. Then their moms had become best friends too, which might have been the girls' plan all along.

Everything was changing this year though. Gemma's mom, Mrs. White, was a Spanish immersion teacher and, in the fall, would start working at a new school, Riverwoods Academy. Gemma was switching there with her.

Maven had thought that the summer might make the sadness of attending different schools less terrible. But things didn't turn out as she'd planned. Gemma's family had a busy schedule. They were traveling to soccer tournaments in South Carolina, Virginia, and even Washington, DC.

Instead of weeks together, the friends had just a few days here and there. They only went to the pool once. And to make matters worse, it had rained.

The day that Gemma left for her first soccer tournament, Maven had moped all day. Until she noticed her brother, Gabriel, was bored too.

Maven decided to plan a summer camp for Gabriel and other young kids in their neighborhood. It was mostly her brother and their cousins, but it had been a success, judging by the glowing entries in her journal.

Her journal, more like a scrapbook, was fat with pictures she and the kids had drawn, photos of their adventures, and notes of things she could improve next year.

Looking back was better than looking ahead.

Just thinking of fifth grade without Gemma made butterflies tickle her stomach.

"Knock, knock," her mom said from the door.

Maven never closed it. The sounds of her parents still awake gave her more comfort than a lullaby. But it was nice that her mom didn't just barge into her room.

"Can I come in?"

"Of course!" Maven said, sitting up.

Her mom sat next to her. Maven loved these moments to catch up right before bed. Her mom was a nighttime nurse. The schedule worked because Maven's dad was a librarian, and so one of them was usually home. Even though the love-filled one-on-ones with her mom were brief, Maven still looked forward to them.

After one of their nightly charlas—talks—she always fell asleep with a smile and never had bad dreams.

"The triplets were so excited, Mavencita! Good job!"

Maven's face glowed. "Look at what Gabriel drew."

Her mom took the paper Maven offered. She looked at the drawing of the meadow turned into a fairy citadel. Her face shone with pride.

"He's becoming quite the artist!" she said. "Thanks to that watercolor class you suggested at the beginning of the summer, he's just bloomed! He learned a lot."

Maven shrugged. "He has a passion for drawing. I just introduced a different way he could express it. I love how he imagines Magicstan."

"Magicstan!" Mami exclaimed, and laughed, but not in a mocking way. "You have a passion for storytelling! I don't know how you do it."

Maven couldn't hide her smile. She did have a love for stories. Losing herself in her imagination was her favorite thing in the world. Which seemed cool to the little kids and the grown-ups, but . . . would her friends think so too? What would they say once they went back to school and Maven was still stuck on the same thing she'd liked since kindergarten?

Gemma wouldn't be there anymore to act as a human bridge between Maven and the cooler kids.

The tickles in Maven's tummy turned painful.

She knew this feeling well, and she didn't like it.

When she was little, she called these nerves "the scaries."

"Most of all I love that you're comfortable in your own skin, and that you're true to yourself," Mom said, kissing her forehead.

"Hmmm, you think?" Maven asked. She didn't feel as comfortable in her own skin as her mom made it sound.

"Of course! Don't ever lose that, Mavencita. Don't grow up!" She looked at the clock on the wall and said, "Look at the time! Off to bed. Tomorrow will be a long and busy day, and you need to rest."

She kissed Maven on the forehead and left.

"Chau, chau, Mami," Maven said, and went to bed.

But once under the covers, Maven stayed up looking at the ceiling. Soon enough, her mind started making connections among the things that had happened throughout the day. But unlike every night, it wasn't a story that was lulling her to sleep.

She worried more and more as the clock ticked the passing seconds, feeding the scaries.

Her mom had meant well, but Maven wasn't all

that comfortable in her own skin. She wanted to grow up. She wanted to be like everyone else.

When people thought of Gabriel, they thought of his art. Grey was obsessed with dinosaurs. Valentina liked ballet, and Ruby loved gymnastics. Gemma now had soccer. Maven liked storytelling and make-believe universes. But if this was all she liked, would her friends think she was still a little kid?

Hopefully fifth grade would be the year she became cool once and for all.

Chapter Two

For Maven, the morning of the first day of school had always been more exciting than Christmas Eve. This day, though, her excitement was tinged with nerves. The scaries hadn't disappeared overnight. If anything, they'd even turned from butterflies to wasps. And with wasps, the only way to avoid being stung was to ignore them and turn in the opposite direction.

"Fifth grade, here I come!" she exclaimed, and jumped out of bed. She got dressed lightning fast before the scaries got ahold of her again. The night before, she had prepared her outfit: embroidered jeans, a flowery shirt, and green sneakers.

Her brand-new pink canvas backpack waited by the door. She only had to grab her matching pink lunchbox from the fridge, and she was ready to roll.

When she opened the door of her room, she found herself face-to-face with a wide-eyed, bright-cheeked Gabriel. He looked super sharp in his short-sleeve button-up shirt and cargo shorts. His white sneakers were gleaming. His hair was aggressively tamed with a blob of gel, but he had a curl sticking up in the back, like a little antenna.

"Let me help you," she said.

His shoulders dropped in relief. "Thanks! I've been trying and trying, but that curl won't budge! Why don't I have straight hair like you?"

It wasn't the first time he complained about his hair. The siblings looked very much alike, with skin bronzed by the sun and big brown eyes. But her long mahogany hair was straight like a board, and his was tightly curled. She wished she had his, and he wished he had hers.

"Come here," she said, and led him to the bathroom at the end of the hallway. She wet her hand in the sink and patted down his hair, trying to smooth over the glommed gel in the front of his head. She had a small comb in one of her backpack pockets, and after a couple of strokes, his hair was tamed down as he wanted.

"There," she said.

He inspected her work in the mirror for a split second and finally nodded. "Awesome. Thank you, Mav!" Gabriel turned and looked at Maven in that suspicious way of his. "How come you know how to do everything?"

She laughed, her cheeks warming up. "I don't know how to do everything! What are you talking about?"

He rolled his eyes. "Fine. Don't tell me how. But one day, I'll figure it out."

"Kids! Hurry up! We don't want to be late on the first day of school!" Papi called from the kitchen.

Maven and Gabriel beamed at each other.

The wasplike scaries took a little nap as she followed her brother down the stairs.

The school principal and the teachers rolled out the red carpet to welcome the students.

Literally.

Besides an actual red carpet, there was a photo

booth, balloons, music, and snacks. It was a party. Maven loved parties. Well, planning them, actually. When she was in charge, she knew how to keep herself occupied, but now, she lingered by her dad's side.

Once Gabriel saw his friends, he dashed to meet them, though not before their dad snapped a quick picture to send to Mom, who was still at work.

Finally, Maven kissed her dad on the cheek, and she too went to find her friends. She wished Gemma, her number one, were here. Such a bummer not to share the last year of elementary together. Luckily, they had Girl Scouts later in the week.

Maven looked all over for familiar faces. Some people had really changed during the summer. Finally, she spotted someone from her Girl Scout troop. Zahara had always been one of the tallest girls in their class, and she'd grown even more during the summer. She was impossible to miss among all the kids crowding around the school entrance.

"Zahara!" Maven called out.

Zahara, who was quiet and reserved, turned around in surprise and returned Maven's smile. "Oh, hi, Maven!"

There was a pause that soon edged on uncomfortable.

Maven's mind raced as she thought of how to keep the conversation going, but then Zahara said, "You look . . . taller?"

Maven's chest filled with a pleasant glow. Maybe her fears of being seen as a little kid had been all for nothing.

"Thanks!" Maven replied. "I . . . I love your new backpack! Where did you get it?"

At Maven's words, Zahara broke into a smile almost as bright as the rhinestone constellations that decorated her backpack.

"Thanks, I got it in Florida when we went to visit NASA."

"NASA? Like, the actual place?" Maven exclaimed. "That's so . . . cool!"

She tried to think very fast on what else to say, but she knew nothing about NASA. Finally, she asked, "What was your favorite thing about it?"

"Oh! I loved so many things! But let me start at the beginning," Zahara said. As she talked, her eyes lit up, and she made enthusiastic expressions with her hands like words weren't enough to express how much she'd loved the visit.

Obviously, Zahara had been bursting with desire for someone to ask her this question. The shy and reserved girl turned into a whole other person. Once she got going about her family's road trip to Florida, she didn't stop. Maven had never seen Zahara so animated. She shared how fun it was to see the countryside and city after city zip by through the window, the thrill of arriving at NASA in time to see the launching of a shuttle heading to the moon, and even how delicious the pineapple ice cream was at the amusement parks.

"And the beach! Ah!" said Zahara. "It was perfect, even though I got a sunburn." The skin on her freckled nose was still peeling. Her sunburn must have been so painful!

By the time she had run out of steam—and words— more kids from their grade had arrived. All around the girls, kids chatted excitedly about their summers in little groups of twos and threes. Maven caught snatches of their conversations.

One of the boys had also been in Florida, while several had visited their families in Puerto Rico, Mexico, and Colombia. Emilee had been camping in Yellowstone and she wouldn't stop talking about all the other national parks she wanted to visit. Jane had gone to New York to sing with the children's choir she was a part of, and even Ariel, who was in fourth grade but liked to hang out with the older kids, chimed in to tell anyone who'd listen about the slime shop she'd set up with her brother. Apparently, they were making bank.

At first, Maven was going to tell Zahara and the rest about her homemade summer camp and the stories she'd made up about Magicstan for her brother and the triplets. But the more she listened to her classmates, the more that plan crumbled.

She might be a little taller, but, she was still the same Maven as ever.

Who'd want to listen to made-up stories about a make-believe place? When she really thought about it, compared to everyone's real-life adventures, her summer seemed *so* childish.

The scaries came back with a vengeance.

This time around, Maven couldn't shoo them away with a smile or positive thoughts.

Things didn't get better once the bell rang and they

headed inside. Everyone was excited after the rush of meeting friends and feasting on fancy sprinkled doughnuts. Although Maven's new teacher, Mrs. Wagner, had told her class to line up a few feet from the door, everyone tried to rush in at once to get the best seat.

Without Gemma to guide her, Maven wasn't sure if the coolest place in fifth grade would be in the front or the back of the class. She found a seat in the middle. It's not like she didn't have any friends. It's just that she'd always stuck with Gemma, and everyone else was already paired up with their best friend.

There were only two empty desks, including the one next to her that would've been Gemma's. Who else was missing? Oh, Reyker, a boy who'd always been nice to her. He had moved before the end of last year. Maven resigned herself to sitting next to an empty desk.

Until a new girl came in. Curly blond hair framed her slightly pinched face. Maven recognized the frantic look in the girl's eyes even though she wore glasses. The girl looked like a toad in a new pond, as her dad sometimes said.

It was exactly how Maven felt, and she'd known these kids all her life!

Maven smiled, and the girl smiled back. Quickly, she rushed to claim the remaining seat next to Maven. Not a moment too soon, since Mrs. Wagner walked into the classroom and closed the door.

"Hi! I'm Maven," she whispered.

The girl opened her mouth to reply, but Mrs. Wagner started speaking to the class.

"Welcome to a new school year! I'm so excited for all the adventures we'll have." She had that same no-nonsense way about her that Maven's mom had—like someone who got things done without wasting time. She was tall and strong. Her dark brown hair was shoulder-length, and her nails were polished like a rainbow.

"Most of you met me during back-to-school night last week, but just to remind you, I'm passionate about reading, teaching, and football, in that order."

Maven smiled with relief. She already liked Mrs. Wagner. Apart from football, they had interests in common.

Before Maven could ask her what her favorite book was, Ben asked, "What's your favorite team?"

When Mrs. Wagner replied with something Maven

didn't understand, some kids cheered and others rolled their eyes. But soon they all settled down to work on the first assignment: "Tell me about your summer."

Maven, who in the past had been so excited to share her writing with her class, suddenly felt shy. She'd been hoping that the conversation would move beyond what they had done during the break. Not because her family hadn't been on a fancy vacation or a cool camping trip, but because for the first time in her life, she worried her pastime of making up activities to entertain her brother and cousins seemed so boring.

What if her classmates made fun of her? And what would the new girl think of her?

Maven doubted the new girl would think she was one of the cool fifth graders.

So she wrote about a fun day at the community pool when they'd celebrated the triplets' birthday. That had been during the mermaid section of her camp.

In her narration, she didn't include the scavenger hunt or the stories about Sirenalandia (a magical place filled with mermaids and singing fish) that had consumed Gabe and the triplets for weeks.

Even though Maven looked a little taller, at least to

Zahara, it seemed her class had moved on to more mature things while she was stuck in a make-believe land.

Nervously, she chewed on the top of her pencil
while she hoped Mrs. Wagner wouldn't call on her to
read aloud.

Chapter Three

Thank goodness Mrs. Wagner didn't call on anyone to share their summer reports aloud. She said she'd read them and return them in a couple of days.

"Now it's time for the math review!" she announced.

A chorus of groans rippled across the room. Never in her life had Maven been excited for a math review, but now she didn't complain about the pages and pages of multiple-choice problems that tested how much she remembered from last year.

She had a good memory, and the scaries quieted for a bit. But when it was time for subtracting fractions, she started sweating.

Luckily, the lunch bell came to the rescue.

Good timing, if the growl of many stomachs was an indication.

"Even I needed a break!" Zahara said on the way out the classroom.

Zahara loved math, but it always took some time to get used to sitting in a classroom for so long after summer vacation.

Maven, lunch box in hand, and the rest of her class headed outside. She sat down under a tree with a few girls she knew to enjoy her bento box. But soon after they were done eating, people started pairing up and forming into groups for recess games or just to talk. Without Gemma to pull her along, Maven was soon standing alone under the shade of the magnolia tree. A few yards away, the new girl stood looking at some boys playing four square. The longing to join them was clear on her face. But that group of boys was highly competitive, and they didn't like to lose even at recess games. The only girl they'd ever let join was Gemma, who never took no for an answer anyway and negotiated for the girls to play too.

But without her around, it seemed playground politics had gone back to being unfair.

Maven wondered what kind of person the new girl was. Finally, she gathered the courage and walked up to get to know her.

"Hi! Sorry we couldn't talk in class. You're new this year, right?" she asked.

She realized Mrs. Wagner hadn't singled out the new girl either or made her introduce herself in front of the whole class like other teachers had in the past. Another reason she liked her new teacher.

"I'm Sylvie," the new girl said. "And yes, we—I mean—my family and I moved from South Carolina to Savannah last week."

"Last week? Wow! What have you been doing so far? Do you like it here?" Maven realized she'd asked so many things at once, and added, "Sorry! I get carried away sometimes."

Sylvie smiled back. "I like it here. It looks a lot like home, even. But I really don't know anyone yet, so . . . it's been kind of boring," she said, casting her eyes down to the ground as if a clue of what to say next lay hidden in the clover patch.

Maven had lived in the same house and attended the same school all her life. She had never been *the new girl*, but she recognized a little bit of Sylvie's lone-liness because she had felt it too. For the first time in her life, she felt distant from the kids she'd known for years. She couldn't even imagine what it would be like to start all over again. She wondered how Gemma was doing at her new school, being the new girl. But then, Gemma always fit into place anywhere she landed.

"What do you like to do? Do you play sports?" she asked.

"Yes and no . . . I played soccer back in South Carolina," Sylvie said, and then she chuckled. "But since our move was kind of last-minute, I'm too late to join a team. Everyone had tryouts early in the summer, you know?"

Maven remembered how nervous Gemma had been during tryouts season. The worry had been for nothing. Naturally, she'd made the team. The two of them had gone to the ice cream shack to celebrate after the coach had posted the roster on the team's web-site. Maven had been happy for Gemma, of course, but she'd also been so relieved not to have to go through that kind of process to get to do what she loved. She couldn't imagine the pressure.

And to make the team and then move away? Brutal!

"My friend Gemma is on a traveling soccer team. She's awesome! You should meet her! Maybe she can get you onto the team." Maven didn't know if Gemma could actually help, but she wanted Sylvie to feel better.

"I'd love that," Sylvie said.

"Gemma doesn't go here anymore," Maven said, and her words sounded like an apology.

Sylvie's smile dropped for the blink of an eye, but she didn't falter. Instead, she continued the conversation. "What about you? What do you like to do?"

"I . . ."

Maven's scaries prickled her.

She was going to say that she loved setting up activities for little kids, but she didn't want Sylvie to think she was boring. She wished there was something awesome she could share about herself. Something cool. Maybe then she and the new girl could become best friends, but before she could think of something to say, the bell rang again.

This time, the sound was disappointing. Her time had run out before she and Sylvie could get to know each other better.

Sylvie seemed to read this on her face and said, "Let's talk more later. Good thing we're desk neighbors!"

Maven felt energized by her enthusiasm as they walked into the classroom.

But when Mrs. Wagner went over the science class objectives and goals for the year, the post-lunch tiredness set in.

Everyone was quiet but not really paying attention to what their teacher said, judging by the vacant looks on some of the kids' faces. Out of the corner of her eye, Maven saw Dominic try to hide a yawn.

Maven rested her head on her fist, her elbow on the desk while her mind whirred with ideas on what she wanted to be known for. Something that would make her interesting and cool. Something no one expected from her.

What could it be?

"I know it's a lot to remember for the first day of school," Mrs. Wagner was saying. "But hopefully tackling all these systems now will help us get ready for our school district's annual fifth-grade robotics tournament. Our first unit in science is electricity and magnetism, which is perfect to set up the foundation for robotics."

Robotics tournament? Maven sat up. She knew nothing about robots, but she could learn, couldn't she? And robots were the future, after all. Most important, robots were something concrete. Something more mature than making up stories about nonexistent fairylands and creating activities around them.

She was all ears.

Sensing her interest, Mrs. Wagner continued, her gaze often returning to Maven. "It's a class project, but we need a leader to represent our class. That means keeping everyone organized and on task in choosing a project and bringing it into completion. Any volunteers?" She smiled widely as her gaze traveled over the room. She obviously didn't anticipate what followed.

Total silence.

The only one who appeared uncomfortable by the pause seemed to be Maven. Maybe because she was the only one really paying attention.

Unable to resist the pull of this opportunity, Maven jumped to her feet and exclaimed, "I'll do it!" She put her hand up in the air for more emphasis. Her heart pounded hard as she realized the whole class was looking at her with a mixture of surprise and curiosity. "I volunteer as a leader." Her voice was a thin thread by the end of her words.

"Are you sure, Maven?" asked Sawyer, one of the boys who'd been playing four square, with an infuriating smirk.

"Yes. Why?" Maven asked, starting to regret her rush to volunteer.

Sawyer was famous for his obsession with fishing. He even wore his fishing vest to school. Last year the principal had expressively forbidden him from carrying worms in his pockets. Maven hadn't expected Sawyer to object to her. If someone would, she'd have expected that person to be Zahara, but the astronomy-obsessed girl was furtively reading a book about supernovas hidden under her desk.

Sawyer didn't reply, so Maven insisted. "Do *you* want to do it?"

The class—minus Zahara—acted like they were watching a tennis match, their eyes swiveling from Maven to Sawyer. Finally, something had shaken them from the post-lunch daze.

"Me? What? No, but . . ."

"But what?"

Sawyer blushed all the way to his ears. "It's just that . . . it's *robotics*!" He chuckled and looked around the room for support.

Some of the boys nodded in agreement with him.

"So?" A person that had never spoken up in their classroom broke the awkward silence. It was Sylvie, the new girl. "Why can't Maven lead a project about robotics?"

"You don't know her. Let's just say that no one thinks robots are Maven's specialty," Isaac chimed in, jumping to his buddy's defense. He and Sawyer were inseparable. Maven felt ridiculous. Even though she hadn't shared about her summer of babysitting, the whole class thought she wasn't cool.

The atmosphere turned tense suddenly. Or maybe Maven's feelings were starting to spread all around her.

Voices rippled across the room as more people gave their opinion. The volume rose and rose. But not as much as the doubts in Maven's mind.

Maybe Isaac had a point. Maybe Maven had spoken up too soon. Maybe this was a recipe for disaster.

Contrary to her brother's belief, this was proof that Maven didn't know everything. In fact, she knew nothing.

Maven felt herself crumple like a piece of paper. The scaries squirmed in her stomach until she regretted eating the extra hard-boiled egg in her bento box.

Resolutely, Sylvie stood up and faced the teacher. "Mrs. Wagner, does the leader have to be an expert in robotics to volunteer?"

Every eye was fixed on the teacher, who seemed to be enjoying the whole thing.

"Absolutely not," she said in a voice like those judges on TV morning shows. "I don't know the first thing about robots myself, although, one of my favorite family members is the automatic vacuum that runs at night when we're all asleep!"

"We have one of those!" Sawyer mumbled and shrugged one shoulder.

Maven had no idea what he and the teacher were talking about. Were there really robots that vacuumed at night when everyone was asleep? Lucho would keep the whole family up with his barks. The dog and the vacuum were sworn enemies.

Mrs. Wagner continued, "But that's the point of the project: learning! We all will learn together, right?"

"But why does a *girl* have to be the leader?" Dominic asked. He was a quiet boy, but he was the boys' leader, the one who'd ultimately agreed to Gemma joining their four square game.

The way he said *girl* made even Mrs. Wagner bristle.

Since when did being a boy or a girl affect what people could or couldn't do? Maven had doubts because she wasn't into electronics or robotics but not because she was a girl!

"And why not?" their teacher asked. "Do you want to volunteer too?"

Dominic's face reddened, and he whispered something Maven didn't catch.

Silence fell in the classroom.

"Okay, then, let's vote," Mrs. Wagner said. "We have a lot more to cover before the end of the day, and I'd love for this to be resolved as soon as possible."

All of a sudden, Maven felt the stakes of her decision to volunteer grow monumentally. Maybe she should withdraw herself from this mess. If things went wrong with the project, then she'd be letting down her class, her teacher, and worse, the girls.

But it was too late to step back.

Mrs. Wagner said, "Those in favor of Dominic being our leader, put your hands up."

Most of the boys raised their hands without hesitation, but a couple of them looked around as if they didn't know what to do. Dominic sent them a desperate glance, and reluctantly, they too voted for Dominic, which seemed to be a vote of confidence for the boys' team.

A shadow of sadness —or was it disappointment? —crossed Mrs. Wagner's face, but she didn't interfere.

"Now, those for Maven," she said.

Maven was trying to count the hands up in the air, but she was a little emotional seeing that all the girls were voting for her. She hadn't expected that.

Sylvie sent her an encouraging look as she kept her hand up.

"She's only winning because there are more girls," Dominic muttered.

Right! With Sylvie, the number of students were uneven! Maven wasn't sure how to feel about this, but one thing was certain. She couldn't let the girls down.

"It's decided, then! Maven is our official fifth-grade robotics team leader." The girls broke into cheers, but Mrs. Wagner added, "And Dominic will be her helper."

Maven sent Dominic a friendly smile, hoping they could make their peace. But he shook his head as he groaned. "Just what I needed on the first day of school. Brilliant, Ortiz. Bravo. I hope you're happy."

Chapter Four

The final bell rang, but Maven couldn't stop thinking about the mess she put herself into. She was sure social studies was important, but in this moment, she could think only of robotics.

What did robotics even mean? Was Maven expected to invent one of those automatic vacuums Mrs. Wagner loved so much? Maybe she'd get more information on Friday. Mrs. Wagner had told her and Dominic that there would be a meeting for all class representatives with a coordinator from the school district.

What if everyone else was a robotics genius?

Even the scaries were scared into silence at how impossible the task seemed.

All around her, people were dashing to the exit.

Maven's first instinct was to talk to Mrs. Wagner and tell her she had made a mistake, but the teacher was chatting with Zahara.

"Are you okay?" Sylvie asked as she gathered her things in her backpack.

Maven looked up at her. "Yes, thanks for speaking up for me."

"Well, that boy was rude." Sylvie rolled her eyes.

"I just don't know what mess I got myself into," Maven confessed after making sure no one was around them.

Seeing how surprised Sylvie was at her words, she regretted saying anything. She forgot she wanted to look cool to the new girl and not insecure like this.

"I think you will be perfect." Sylvie paused. "I can help you."

"What? Are you an expert on robots or something?" she asked as they headed to the hallway together.

Sylvie smiled, crunching her nose. "No, but like Mrs. Wagner said, we can learn."

She was right.

Gratitude bloomed in Maven's chest, and she hoped Sylvie could see she really meant it. "Thank you."

She wanted to do something nice for Sylvie.

If the day had been long and intense for Maven, she couldn't even imagine what Sylvie must be feeling. Arriving at a new school during the last year of elementary had to be one of the hardest things ever. Learning new ways of doing things, figuring people out, trying to remember concepts from last year. She had to be exhausted!

Sylvie seemed like she was social and outgoing. She didn't know anyone in the area. All groups, cliques, and even competitive teams were established. The only other place that was perfect to meet new friends was—

"Would you like to come to my Girl Scouts meeting tomorrow? You can meet Gemma there."

Sylvie looked unconvinced, and Maven added, "I think you two will get along great. She's super funny *and* fun. You both can come to my house after the meeting, and we can all hang out."

Sylvie didn't reply right away. In fact, at the mention of Girl Scouts, it looked like she was trying not to roll her eyes. "Girl Scouts? I don't know. . . ."

That wasn't the reaction Maven had been going for.

Sylvie swallowed. Her cheeks were bright red when she said, "It's just that my mom suggested we find a troop. My older sister who's in college loved it when she was my age, but I'm not sure I want to be the new girl there like I am at school."

Maven understood Sylvie's hesitation. She'd too been nervous about joining the troop when Gemma had suggested they join. But once she'd met the leaders, and the girls, she'd loved it. She always had so much fun.

"I mean, Girl Scouts is a perfect place to meet friends. We go on field trips, and meet a lot of interesting people, like last year a former astronaut came to talk to us!"

That was Zahara's love-of-space origin story.

Sylvie glanced toward a group of other girls talking, her longing like a mask.

Quickly, before she lost her attention, Maven added, "A lot of girls from the area attend, not just our school, so we can get to know them before we're all together in middle school next year."

Maybe it was the enthusiasm in Maven's voice or maybe she was actually eager to meet Gemma. The fact is, Sylvie finally smiled and said, "And your friend, the famous Gemma, is in the troop too, you said?"

"Yes! We've been in the same troop since we were little."

"Okay," Sylvie said. "I'll try it."

"Cool," Maven said, giving her a high five. "We meet at the Pleasant Meadows library every Tuesday after school." She got a paper and a pencil from her desk and wrote her mom's number. "Just in case you have questions, you can call me."

Suddenly she realized that not having a phone was the epitome of being uncool, but it was too late to pull the words back.

Sylvie's cheeks turned bright red again, but not because she was embarrassed for Maven. "Um . . . I don't have a phone," she said. "I must be the only fifth grader without her own phone in the whole wide world."

Maven shrugged, trying to tamp down her relief at not being the last girl in the no-phone club. "I don't have my own phone either. This is my mom's number."

"So you know how it feels!"

"Totally!" said Maven, and she skipped all the way to her dad's car waiting in the carpool lane.

Chapter Five

That night after the longest first day of school ever, Maven's parents assured her she'd do an excellent job being the project leader for her class. Gabriel echoed their words.

But she didn't feel that confident. She was happy all the girls had voted for her. But not one single boy believed she was up to the task. If she failed, she'd prove them right. She'd never hear the end of it. She would cry in front of the whole class, and how would that make her look cool and mature? They'd think she was a baby. A baby who failed.

Maven was too nervous over the whole thing to even attempt to pour her feelings into her journal. What if it fell into the wrong hands? She'd seen too many TV shows and read too many books to not know this was a possibility. So instead, the scaries grew and gnawed at her stomach until she fell asleep, all through the night, and into the next school day.

In the morning, when Maven asked her more details about the project, Mrs. Wagner said, "The representative from the district will go over the rules of the competition and such on Friday. But we can get a little head start. In all my years I've learned that you can't be too prepared."

"That's right," Maven said.

Dominic huffed and rolled his eyes.

Mrs. Wagner must have not seen his reaction, or maybe she decided to let it pass. She continued, "Everyone should start researching on robotics before we decide what our class will build. I compiled a list of books and websites that are informative. You will find at least one copy of each book in the media center here at school. Your first task will be to split up the list into five groups. Good luck, kids! Now off you go."

Maven turned to Dominic, paper in hand, and said, "I'll split up the groups." That's something she knew she could do.

He just shrugged and said, "You can divide it how-ever you like. I don't care."

Maven also wanted to go ahead and check out as many books as she could before they were all gone, but Dominic was already trudging back to their classroom.

A few minutes later, she stood in front of the whole class, trying to hide that she was shaking like a leaf, and said, "You get who you get, and you don't get upset."

She regretted her words instantly. This phrase al-ways worked like a charm. With four-year-olds. Her classmates didn't take kindly to it—or her—though. There was so much complaining that Mrs. Wagner had to intervene.

No one seemed to be happy with the groups, and Maven fought hard to hold back her tears all morning.

As she had feared, when Maven made her way back to the media center, all the available copies of the books had been claimed. The media specialist told her they were available digitally, but Maven preferred to read physical books.

She'd get them from the county library. Another reason to look forward to Girl Scouts.

She couldn't wait to see Gemma and introduce her to Sylvie too, of course.

Later, during the last recess, Maven saw Sylvie watching Dominic, Sawyer, and the rest of the boys playing four square, taking over the whole playground. It wasn't fair. But no one complained. This was way more unjust than being assigned to a random group for a project. Why was no one calling the boys out?

When the final bell rang, Maven couldn't contain her enthusiasm for finally meeting her friends. She caught up with Sylvie and asked, "Do you want to walk to the library together?"

It was only a short walk. About two blocks.

Sylvie said, "My mom wants to drive me. Meet you there?"

Maven tried to hide her disappointment, but she could walk with Zahara and Ariel, who was also in the troop. And that's what she did.

When the girls, thirsty and hot, arrived at the library's meeting room, their troop leaders, Maggie and Vanessa, had just finished setting everything up. Snacks and drinks were banned everywhere else in the library, but in the teen-area meeting room, they had a green a light.

"Welcome!" their leaders exclaimed when the girls walked into the room.

One by one, the rest of the troop trickled in. Most of the catching up had happened at school, and thank goodness, Vanessa and Maggie were more interested in hearing about the beginning of school than how the summer had gone. Already, Maven felt more relaxed than at school.

If only Gemma would arrive already! But she knew too well that her BFF always ran a few minutes later than the rest of the world.

Maven poured herself a cup of water as she looked out the window into the park and the street beyond the trees. A family of squirrels frantically ran up and down a giant pine tree, carrying something in their mouths. Winter seemed a long time from now, but squirrels planned ahead. Like Mrs. Wagner said, it was better to be prepared. The squirrels were smart little things. Maven sighed, thinking that she had a lot of things in common with preschoolers, teachers, and squirrels. Not so much with her classmates.

She spotted Sylvie heading toward the library, and her heart leaped inside her. She ran to meet her new friend before anyone else could beat her to it.

"Sylvie!" she exclaimed. "You came!"

"Hi," Sylvie said, waving shyly at the leaders and the girls already claiming their spots on the sofas and beanbags scattered around.

"Hey, all!" a mischievous voice called out. "Did you miss me?"

"Gemma!" everyone yelled in unison.

Gemma might be everyone's favorite, but Maven knew she was Gemma's number one. She wasn't wrong. Gemma smiled at everyone, but she beelined in Maven's direction.

They hugged like they hadn't seen each other in a million years. It's not like Maven kept track of the days, but they'd never been apart for so long.

"I have so much to tell you!" they both said at the same time, jumping with excitement and accidentally bumping into Sylvie, who still had a foot on either side of the door, as if she hadn't completely made up her mind about staying or not.

Maven remembered her manners.

"Gemma! This is Sylvie. She's new to Pleasant Meadows," Maven said. "Sylvie, this is my best friend, Gemma!"

There's something special in claiming someone as *your* best friend, and Maven's chest always glowed with warmth when she said this phrase.

Sylvie and Gemma smiled at each other as they walked through the door. Immediately, the rest of the troop swarmed around Gemma, trying to catch up too. They'd missed her at school!

It had been like this forever. Everywhere Gemma went, it was like she had a personal spotlight that followed her around. Sometimes, Maven even swore she could see the light bouncing off Gemma's curls. Maven loved that about her, especially because Gemma always shone her light on everyone else, making them feel special.

Maven quickly introduced Sylvie to the rest of the group, and everyone, including the leaders, welcomed her warmly.

Sylvie sat next to Gemma and asked, "I heard you like soccer. What position do you play?" Her eyes were shiny as she looked at Gemma.

The two of them chatted about soccer until Maggie, Gemma's aunt, and Vanessa opened the meeting.

Maven loved the familiar structure. She had a little card with the Girl Scout Promise and Law in her journal, and she passed it to Sylvie so she could follow along while the rest of the group recited it by heart.

"Welcome, everyone, and especially Sylvie, our guest!" Maggie said. She had a way of looking at every girl and making her feel like she was the most incredible person ever. Maven loved that about her. "I'm so happy to have you all here again!"

"I missed you all so much!" Vanessa said. "How's the first week of school been?"

Maven wanted to share that, without her best friend, school had been so difficult. But Gemma raised her hand first. Vanessa nodded at Gemma to open the floor to venting.

"The first week has been intense! I knew a couple of kids from soccer, so I have some friends already, but they do everything backward at that school! Lunch is a whole hour later than at my other school, and the cafeteria is really far from the playground."

Maven couldn't help feeling a twinge of jealousy

that Gemma already had found friends when she'd been struggling so much without her.

"I know how that feels," Sylvie said, sighing deeply. "They do a different kind of math here, and it's just hard to understand. It's so unfair that I didn't get a better score on the review."

There was a rumble of agreement among the girls.

Gemma and Sylvie exchanged a look of partners-in-suffering at new schools.

By now, other girls had raised their hands to share about their first week of school and the end of their summer.

In her seat, Maven squirmed. She struggled these last few days, but she'd known her classmates, the schedule, and the layout of the school for most of her life. Being a new kid sounded terrible. She didn't feel like sharing her feelings anymore when others had it so much worse. After a few minutes, Vanessa said, "Thank you to those who shared. Now, are you ready to hear what's next?"

The girls cheered.

"According to the plans you girls made before the summer break," Maggie said, "we have a great deal of incredible things lined up this fall."

"Aquarium time, baby!" Gemma exclaimed, and jumped up from her seat with her hands in the air.

Everyone laughed.

"Yes, Gemma, the aquarium visit is first on our list!" Maggie said.

Maven gently grabbed her friend's hand and pulled her back to her seat.

Maven loved how organized their troop was. The girls had voted on the activities they wanted to do and worked together to plan them. Truth be told, Maven had learned a lot of her planning skills during troop meetings.

The aquarium was in Garden City, which was about fifteen minutes away from their neighborhood, and had just reopened after a big renovation.

"You're going to love it," Maven whispered to Sylvie.

"Yes, you are!" Gemma added.

A buzzing of excited chatter spread among the girls as they all shared what they were looking forward to the most. Anika was practically glowing. Visiting the aquarium had been her idea last year. She loved animals—even those she couldn't cuddle with, like fish—and knew more about them than anyone else in the troop. She could even name the different kind of birds that visited her mom's garden during the different seasons.

Maggie continued giving them the details about how this project would help them work toward earning their STEAM patch. STEAM stood for science, technology, engineering, arts and mathematics.

"Vanessa and I aren't experts in aquatic life, but we're excited to learn with you all."

All of a sudden, Maven's nerves about volunteering to lead the robotics project at school lessened. After all, this was exactly what Mrs. Wagner had also said. They could all learn together.

Maven would've never chosen robotics as a hobby she wanted to excel at, but maybe all things happened for a reason. She saw herself fifteen years in the future commandeering a fleet of robots . . . but what kind, exactly? Why were robots even a part of life? Who had come up with the first idea for them, after all?

There was so much she didn't know, but she

trusted she could learn. A few years ago, she'd known nothing about Girl Scouts, and now she felt at home with this troop that had become a second family.

Vanessa handed out a copy of the STEAM pledge for each girl to sign.

"And I hope you don't forget about it once you put it in your binders," Maggie said.

Maven read the pledge silently.

I pledge to stay curious, to ask questions about how things work and why. I will learn that each failed attempt I make at something will help lead me to a successful outcome, and I will continue to try without being discouraged. . . .

It seemed as if the pledge had been written just for her. It was a powerful reminder that she could face any challenge.

The weeks ahead would be dedicated to things that were out of her comfort zone. When the robotics project became a success, then maybe she'd be one of the cool kids at school once and for all.

Chapter Six

A couple of books Mrs. Wagner had recommended weren't available at the county library. Maven was disappointed she couldn't get them right away. Maybe her dad could find them at the library in the community college where he worked though. That was one of the greatest perks of having a librarian as a dad.

Which made her shake her head at herself again. Why hadn't she volunteered to be a leader of the Battle of the Stories competition? Or even the science fair? Her mom always had the best ideas for science projects. Last year she'd helped Maven and her group with a model of the circulatory system that earned them a special honor mention.

But robots? She was so out of her element!

Still, she had gathered as many books as she could find on robotics. As the project leader, she would have to be even more prepared and knowledgeable than the other kids in her class. Especially Dominic.

She'd seen him climb into his dad's car at the end of the school day, his backpack bursting with books. Dominic wasn't one of the super readers of their class, but he was competitive. He had seen her wave good-bye but had turned his head away as if she were an enemy!

It was obvious that he'd do whatever it took to be better than her. He'd even let her take the blame from dividing the class in groups. She'd never minded Dominic much. Now she couldn't stand even thinking about him.

Maven hoped she was up to the challenge.

"You like robotics and programming, don't you?" said the librarian, Jonah, as he checked out the tottering pile of books Maven had left on the counter.

Maven shrugged and chuckled. "It's for a school project."

In the kids' section, Gemma and Sylvie were laughing. They were sharing a beanbag and cracking up at a book of the world's greatest jokes. They looked like the best of friends already.

Maven had never thought she was the jealous type. After all, she was the one who'd introduced the girls. She knew they'd click like two puzzle pieces, and she was glad she hadn't been wrong. But she still felt an uncomfortable pang. It's not like she could go up to them and ask them to replay all the jokes they'd already laughed about. That would only ruin the fun those two were having. But she had no one else to blame but herself.

Jonah cleared his voice, and Maven's attention came back to the present moment.

"Sorry," she said. "What were you saying?"

"It's great that you're interested in robots. I'm a fan of them," Jonah said.

From the corner of her eye, she saw Gemma sending her a questioning look. If they spent all their time at the library, there wouldn't be time to hang out at Maven's house. Sylvie had to be home by dinner.

But Maven didn't want to appear even ruder when she'd obviously not been paying attention to Jonah.

"How come you're a fan of them?" she asked.

"The scanner that reads the barcode is a robot in a way. When it doesn't work, I have to enter the numbers manually, and my eyesight isn't the best," he said, grinning. His thick bottle-bottom glasses were proof of what he said.

Jonah finished scanning the remaining titles and helped Maven put them in her tote bag. But she had too many to fit in it, so he placed the last two books in a library-branded tote bag from a box next to him.

Maven wanted to leave already, but Jonah continued talking.

"I'm glad I don't have to scan books one by one, and that the return desk has a special way to sort books, so I have more time to do more interesting parts of my job, like helping people find the books they want. Or doing the story time." He looked at his watch, and his eyes widened. "Which reminds me, I need to do the after-school story time! See you later, Maven. And if you need any other titles, you know where to find me."

"Thank you, bye!" she said.

Gemma, who had been sending her more and more alarmed looks by the minute was at Maven's side as soon as Jonah walked away toward the story time area, an octopus hat on his head.

"What took you so long? And what are all these books for?"

Sylvie joined them and asked, "What is he wearing?"

"He was helping me check out books for the robotics project and got carried away talking about the robots that exist in the library."

"Robotics?" asked Gemma.

"Yes," said Maven. "Apparently fifth grade is the year of the big robotics competition across the district."

Gemma's eyes widened with understanding. "Right! I remember my mom saying last year that Mrs. Wagner's class always wins! Who are the team leaders?"

Sylvie pointed at Maven.

Gemma's jaw literally dropped. "What? You? Robotics? That's so funny!"

"Funny?" Maven asked, trying to sound all chill, but when she saw the confusion in Sylvie's eyes, she panicked. Prickly heat climbed up Maven's neck. She could take the boys' lack of confidence in her abilities. And even though she knew Gemma would've voted for her, it bothered her that Gemma seemed to think that Maven being the leader was an outrageous idea. And that she would say so in front of Sylvie.

Maybe Gemma could see all the emotions raging inside of Maven because she added, "I never thought you and robotics would ever be connected, but I guess I was wrong."

Maven shrugged a shoulder like Gemma's words were nothing, but a heavy feeling fell on the little trio.

"How are you going to read all these books?" Sylvie asked as if she were trying to change the mood. "It's not like you have to build a rocket ship on your own!" She said this in a light tone, but there was a look of concern in her eyes.

But then, Gemma exclaimed, "Oh! You don't know our Mavy. She has to be readier than ready, and books are always the first step. Now, let's get going!" Gemma spoke with admiration, and she carried one of the book bags herself as if she were trying to be ultra-supportive. Those were the perks of being friends with the coolest girl in the world. She made you look cool by association.

"I'll help you carry this one, Mavy," Sylvie said. "Do you want me to read these and then give you a summary of what I learned? Some titles were in my group's list."

Maven considered. It's not like she was going to read them all that night, but then, she felt like she had to go through everything first since she was the project leader. And she wanted to prove to Gemma that robotics could be her thing.

"It's okay," she said, taking the bag. "Thank you, though. I'll pass them to you once I'm done with them."

Gemma pretended to cough, and she said something that sounded like "Typical Maven."

Sylvie smiled, and although Maven wanted to smile back, there was something in the back of her mind that stopped her.

Chapter Seven

The walk home wasn't long, but with the heat and humidity, her library haul felt like they were carrying the stone blocks to build the pyramids.

By the time they crossed the last road and the neighborhood was in sight, the three girls were sweaty and tired. And also quiet. There were about a million things to catch up on, but all they could do was gasp for air like fish out of water.

"I could use some lemonade right about now," Maven said, breaking the silence.

"You can say that again," said Sylvie. "I'm—"

A catchy ringtone interrupted her words.

"I thought you didn't have a phone," Maven said. She didn't mean to sound judgy or accusatory. But trying to control her tone of voice was hard when all she could do was breathe.

"It's just my watch," Sylvie said. "I might have caught a random Wi-Fi signal. Hold on." She pressed a button on her watch, and a boy's voice broke out of its tiny speaker.

"Where are you? I've been waiting in front of the library for *hours*."

Sylvie's eyes widened in horror. "Oops." She looked at the girls and said, "It's my brother, Ian. I forgot he was picking me up."

The boy started ranting without taking a breath.

"You'll have to walk now if you don't want me to tell Dad you took off on your own," her brother said. Sylvie cringed and hung up, wiping the sweat from her face with the back of her hand.

"Sorry about that," she said. "He could've given us a ride, but I forgot he was waiting." She shrugged and smiled, all teeth, no amusement at all.

Maven placed a hand on her shoulder and said, "Will you be in trouble? We can walk you to your house and explain."

Sylvie considered it, but then she replied, "It's okay.

I'll have to go home now though. Sorry, I wanted to hang out more." She looked at Gemma when she said this.

Gemma, who had a phone, took it out of her pocket. "No problem. We can hang out another day. What's your watch callback info?"

"My mom has to approve the contacts." Sylvie rolled her eyes.

"Really? That's terrible," Gemma exclaimed.

Maven nodded in understanding. It was terrible, but her situation was even worse. She didn't even have a phone.

"Give me your number and I'll ask her to add you tonight," Sylvie said.

Gemma wrote her name and number on a piece of paper and passed it to Sylvie.

"Do you want us to walk you?" Maven asked.

Sylvie shook her head, handing Maven the bag of extra books. "I live just a block away. And you have all these books. I'll see you tomorrow at school."

"Bye," Sylvie said, waving. "See you tomorrow, Maven. I'll call you, Gemma."

"Yes! Maybe you can come practice with us or something."

Sylvie left, and the friends continued in silence. Maven was bursting to ask what exactly they had talked about, but now that they had another bag of books to carry, talking was even more difficult.

They arrived sweaty and breathless. And to be honest? A little upset.

The triplets and Gabriel were chasing Lucho in circles while Maven's mom watched them from a folding chair she'd placed under the dogwood tree in the front yard. The grass was freshly mowed, its rich, green scent thick in the air. Without hesitation, Gemma dropped the heavy book bag and ran to join them.

Maven's mom grinned at Gemma, who veered sharply and took off in her direction to give her a big hug. Maven felt a little left out, so she placed the two book bags down, and after making sure the water leaking from the hose attached to the faucet wasn't a threat to the books, she joined them.

"Hi, Mavy! What did you do today at Girl Scouts?" Mami asked.

Before Maven could open her mouth, Gemma blurted out, "We're going to the aquarium!"

Mom nodded approvingly. "Nice! Starting with the

STEAM patch, I see. Did you ask Vanessa and Maggie for advice on the robotics competition?"

"Oh no!" Maven said when she realized she'd wasted a perfect opportunity. "I'll ask them next time."

"Since you're trying new things, maybe you should consider giving soccer another chance," Gemma said.

Before Maven could reply, Gemma took off running after Lucho again.

Maven's mom laughed at Gemma's suggestion. She knew her daughter too well.

Maven had never been into soccer. She liked watching games on TV with her family during the World Cup, and she liked to tag along with Gemma's family during the tournaments that lasted all weekend. But from that to actually wanting to play there was a huge gap.

She could learn about robotics. But she had no interest for playing that kind of high-intensity sport.

She looked at her mom, who must have guessed the war going on inside Maven's heart.

"I know that when we're scared of something new, a perfectly normal reaction is wanting to run away from it. Quit before we even start," Mom said. She took a sip of lemonade and offered the glass to Maven, who took a refreshing sip too. "But give robotics a try. You might be surprised."

"Mami, I promise that I'm surprised at myself. What was I thinking?"

Mom laughed again as she fanned herself with her hand. "I'm proud of you for even considering volunteering. You might like it. And who knows? You might end up finding a way to create a robot that mows the lawn."

"Isn't a mower basically that? A robot that mows the lawn? We could get a ride-on lawn mower for Christmas."

"Someone still has to ride the lawn mower though, and instead of doing that, I'd love to spend that time reading."

"You can listen to audio books," Maven countered.

Mami laughed. "You have an answer for everything! That's why I think you're perfect for this. And why you might yet create an automatic lawn mower after all."

"Sure, Mami!" Maven laughed.

"You laugh, but think about it! Not only would the class win the competition, but you'd be rich, Maven!

Every person in the area would want one too. You know how we all cut the lawn so it can grow, so we cut it and it grows, and on and on until the winter."

Right then, something caught Mami's attention, and she looked beyond Maven, who turned around to see what was happening. Gemma had hoisted Valentina on her shoulders and Lucho was going frantic, barking and jumping as if he were trying to save the little girl.

"How do they have the energy?" Mom asked, in awe. "See? If I had a robot to do my chores, then I'd have more energy for fun things."

"I'll look into building you a robot, Mom," said Maven. "That way you won't be so tired."

"Thanks, love. I appreciate the gesture, but, speaking seriously, you don't need to go that big to win the competition, Maven," Mom said kindly.

"What do you mean? Mrs. Wagner's class always wins."

"Right! But since you've never built a robot, maybe you should start with the basics. Like, learn what kind of robots there are. Which one is more feasible to build? And so on."

It was all excellent advice. Yes. The project wouldn't be easy, but she wouldn't quit and let the girls, the whole class, her teacher, and even her troop down. She'd signed the STEAM pledge, after all.

"Come on, Mavy!" Ruby said, grabbing her hand and making her chase Lucho too.

Maven didn't dare place Ruby on her shoulders, she just held her as they ran.

Maven was happy the kids hadn't replaced her with Gemma, who was fast and athletic and over-all fun. Not that she was jealous of her friend, but sometimes, she wished she had a little bit of all her attributes.

The kids eventually got too tired to keep running, and Gemma and Maven were so thirsty they both jumped at Mrs. Ortiz's idea to get more lemonade in the kitchen.

The sun was still high up in the sky, but soon, it would be time for dinner and then getting ready for bed.

"We haven't even really caught up at all," Maven complained, when they both plopped on the leather couch. Maven let Gemma sit in her usual spot just because it was a special occasion.

"We would've been up-to-date if you got that phone already," Gemma complained.

Maven laughed. There was no point arguing. She's told Gemma a thousand times that she wanted one, but her parents had a strict rule of no phones until middle school. "Tell me anyway," Maven insisted.

"Fiiiine," said Gemma, but her eyes were lit up. She took a long breath, and her words unspooled, forming a tapestry of images in Maven's mind. She could practically see the fields where Gemma and her team played tournaments. She could almost imagine the smirk of her new crush (the star goalkeeper of the boys' team), and the pain in Gemma's arm when she got stung by a bee in the middle of a game and she realized she didn't have her EpiPen. Right on the last day of the tournament, she'd had the "mandatory" summer visit to the emergency room that was part of an unwanted "family tradition."

Gemma must have thought Maven's blank look was fear for her because she said, "I didn't even have a big reaction at all." She laughed, but Maven shivered.

"But you had a reaction, no?"

"Yes, but I didn't die!"

"But how could you have left your EpiPen in the hotel! You're extremely allergic to bee stings."

Maven had been with her the day they found out this vital bit of information. They had been four years old, and they were gathering wildflowers for a fairy tea party. It had been the scariest day in Maven's life. She still had nightmares about it and now double-checked there wasn't a bee inside a bloom before she sniffed it.

"It fell from my bag, can you believe it?"

"Were you scared though?" Maven asked, resting her head on Gemma's shoulder in sympathy.

Gemma shrugged. "Not really. The paramedics were so funny, and one made me a glove puppet in the shape of a squirrel. Paramedic and balloon artist! How can a person be so talented?"

Maven bit her lip to stop all the words crowding inside her mouth. How could Gemma be so forgetful? Maven always reminded Gemma to check for the EpiPen in her backpack when they went out exploring in the woods. Just in case. You never knew what could happen!

But Gemma thought it was all a grand adventure.

"What did you do all summer without me, Mavy?"

Gemma asked. "Tell me about your adventures in Magicstan." Her eyes went all dreamy, and she had a sweet smile on her face.

She had loved the games she and Maven played, but one day, she had grown out of them. Still, she didn't make fun of Maven and her storytelling.

Maven rolled her eyes, but she conceded. "Okay . . . if I must."

"Go on!" said Gemma, for once settling down.

"We have a Sirenalandia now in Magicstan," said Maven in her storytelling voice. She went on to describe the different mermaid nations and queendoms, and the history of each group.

Gemma closed her eyes as she listened, her breath deep and steady. Without making a sound, Gabriel and the triplets came in through the back door. Sensing that Maven was telling a story, they too sat quietly by Gemma. Just when Maven was warming up, being herself for the first time since school had started, a car honked outside.

Maven continued the story, and a couple of minutes later, a voice called, "Gemma! Time to go!"

Gemma blinked as if she were waking up from a

trance. One by one, the little kids followed.

Maven sighed, and she had a smile on her face. "That's basically it."

Gemma smiled at her and hugged her. "I've missed you, Mavy! See you next week."

"What about the weekend?" Maven asked, and Gemma shook her head and smiled.

Of course, she had soccer. Her team used the last bit of sunshine and warmth while it lasted before they moved on to indoor practices.

"Okay, see you next meeting. But can I come to your house after?" she asked.

Gemma was already at the door. "Sure! Let's invite Sylvie. I'll text her tonight."

She left before Maven could react. She was craving spending time just with Gemma. They'd spent hours together, but it had all been at the meeting, and then the walk home with Sylvie, and then playing with the kids. They'd had only a few minutes to chat, and Maven was itching with the need to ask Gemma how she did it. How was she so cool and mature that everyone wanted to be her friend? It's not that Maven was jealous or that she didn't like Sylvie. It was that she couldn't just ask this in front of the new friend she wanted to impress.

Since she couldn't ask Gemma right then, she'd worry about another issue. For this question, she had to go to the experts, which were either books or the internet.

"Time for dinner, Mavy," her dad called from the kitchen as he brought two bags full of something that smelled deliciously like empanadas. "Help me set the table?"

"Sure! Papi . . . Can I use the computer after dinner?"

Her dad was plating their food carefully. "What do you need it for? Homework already?"

She nodded her head. "Technically."

"Of course," he said. "Gabriel! Time to eat!"

After dinner, Maven opened the laptop and typed: *What is a robot?*

Chapter Eight

A robot is a machine that can execute a task with little or no human intervention.

Maven clicked on the first link after that, but it looked like a college-level article. She knew most of the words on the screen but not the way they were arranged. The paper seemed to be in a different language altogether.

It all felt like when she tried to read in Spanish.

Her teacher last year had taught the class several ways to narrow searches, so she typed *beginner + robots*. There were fewer results, but still so much material!

She flicked through pages and pages of examples.

Maven's heart started racing again, and her breath

caught in her throat. She felt like she was in one of those dreams in which she showed up to school wearing pajamas, but it was graduation day. Or she had a crazy hairdo, and it wasn't crazy-hair day. Or she had a test and she forgot to study.

"Enough," she said loudly and took a couple of deep breaths.

She felt better.

She grabbed a new notebook and wrote *Robots* on top.

Then she started brainstorming all the kinds of robots she could make. There were so many options.

This would be even harder than she had imagined. The excitement from a few moments before had flattened like a soda left on the counter all day.

But she had made a silent promise to the girls in her class that she could do this, that she could lead the whole team to a victory.

She wasn't going to let them down. This was the greatest challenge of her life, and she wasn't going to give up.

She was Maven Ortiz after all.

Still, this wasn't a project for which she could let

her imagination fly and make up the rules on the go.

The websites agreed on one thing: robotics was a discipline that combined math, design, coding, and planning. Math wasn't her favorite and she had no clue about coding, but she was a good designer, and she knew how to plan and organize.

She wasn't starting from scratch after all.

She'd been told stories ever since she was little, and unconsciously, she'd learned what made a good story, like the characters and structure. Now she had to dig for the basic knowledge of robotics that surely was somewhere in her unconscious, and she'd be golden.

There had to be certain materials used, and measurements, and trials. There might be problems along the way, but she had time.

The class had time, right?

Papi knocked on the door. "Time for bed, Maven."

Maven blinked, but words and diagrams still danced in her eyes. Her shoulders were achy from having been so tensed for so long, and her eyes were strained from looking at the screen for hours.

"Can I have ten more minutes please?"

Papi shook his head. "You can continue tomorrow. Time for bed now. Remember, tomorrow is a new day."

Maven sighed. But he was right. She gave back the computer.

"Can I read for a few minutes?"

Papi sighed, but he gave her a proud smile. He could never say no to more reading time, and they both knew it.

"Okay, but just for a few minutes. I don't want you to be tired for school tomorrow."

"Thanks, Papi. Love you. Good night."

"Good night."

She opened the book at the top of her pile. The one about robots for beginners.

Despite all her plans of getting through one chapter, she read only the first page and fell asleep.

Chapter Nine

On Friday, Mrs. Callahan, from the district, welcomed the fifth-grade class delegates in the school media center. Maven, the only girl, sat in the first row, but the rest took a while to settle. Dominic, who was supposed to be Maven's assistant, finally sat by his friends, two tall boys from his basketball team. He kept pretending Maven didn't exist.

Mrs. Callahan, who looked younger than Maven's mom, explained the rules of the competition for the district in a cheerful and upbeat voice.

But the boys kept laughing behind their hands.

"This is a waste of time," one of them said. "We could've read the information from the flier."

"What does she know about robotics?" another added.

Maven's cheeks burned in secondhand embarrassment. She sat taller to show she was paying attention and being respectful.

"I know it might seem shocking, but I actually started a robotics program at a university. My team in graduate school won an international tournament among fifty countries. I think I know a thing or two about robotics after all," Mrs. Callahan said, in a slightly firmer voice. "Now, raise your hand if you have any background in robotics."

The switch in tone worked. The five boys looked up as if she had called them by name. All but Dominic and Maven raised their hands. Dominic sent Maven a nasty look as if it was her fault the two of them were the only inexperienced ones in the room.

"Excellent," Mrs. Callahan said. "The secret with this project is not thinking you have to build a life-size C-3PO by yourselves."

The boys chuckled, and the tension in the room vanished. But Maven had no idea what she was talking about.

"Having said that, I want to be clear that I don't want your parents building this project for you. The point of the district competition is for fifth graders to learn how to work together with the resources available. Knowledge is a resource in itself."

She passed out little kits for them to redistribute to their classes. "This is a simple bristlebot kit. Go through the instructions, which are extremely simple, and then next week you'll teach it to your class. You can work in pairs now."

Maven's heart sped up with alarm. "You're not going to show us first?"

Mrs. Callahan smiled but shook her head. "If you were younger I would. These are very simple instructions that you can follow." She paused and looked around. "If you work as a team with your partner, you'll be okay."

Dominic exhaled forcefully and looked at the ground.

Maven's hands prickled with sweat. It seemed that getting along with her partner was going to be the most challenging part of the project.

The other two pairs of team leaders started opening

their own kits, and Maven stared at Dominic until he had no choice but to look at her.

Mrs. Callahan pretended not to notice the silent battle going on in front of her. Maybe conflict resolution was a skill the teams would be evaluated on?

"What?" Dominic mouthed at her.

She couldn't believe how stubborn he was. She waved him over, but he shook his head.

"Let's sit here," she whispered, but her voice of course carried all the way to the other boys too. They snickered.

Dominic blushed bright red, but he finally made his way toward her. He sat next to her with a plop that made the chair slide back dangerously.

"Happy?"

"Not really," she said, trying to keep her cool.

He sent her a poisonous look. "I'm here, no?"

She sighed and blew a strand of hair away from her face. "Let's start, because at this point, our class is going to lose. And it's going to be your fault."

Dominic clicked his tongue. "This is stupid. My dad is an engineer, and he says these little competitions are a waste of time. I can ask him to build something that will help us win. You know that's what the other classes will do. That's what it always is."

"You heard the lady from the district. No parent help is allowed. We'll be disqualified."

He shrugged. "They have to say that, but everyone knows no one follows the rules. All the parents help."

Maven had a suspicion he was right, but she was even more stubborn than Dominic.

"I don't care what others do. I'm not going to cheat," she said, opening the kit box.

Dominic didn't argue back, but the stubborn expression on his face spoke louder than words.

"Why don't you read the instructions, and I look at the materials?"

"You're so boring," he said, but he did open the booklet with the instructions.

Maven's skin prickled. *Boring* was the opposite of *cool*. And he, one of the coolest kids in the school, knew what he was talking about.

"I just want to do what I'm supposed to."

"Maybe you could stand as our exhibit for a robot, Ortiz. You just do what you were programmed to do. Do you even think for yourself?"

Maven tried to swallow the knot in her throat. Dominic knew nothing about her.

Thinking was all she did sometimes. Like at that moment, she was thinking she didn't have to take his bad attitude. She'd talk to their teacher and tell her—

Tell her what exactly? That she and Dominic weren't getting along? And what would that solve? If Mrs. Wagner replaced him with another boy from their class, the next one would be just like him, because Dominic was obviously the leader. She'd only be letting down the girls.

No. She had to navigate her way through this situation as if she were circling around a Sirenalandia whirlpool in one of her stories.

She lined up the cut-up toothbrush, the red and yellow thin cables, four tiny wheels, the battery, and a panel with a green backing and a couple of lights.

One of the other two teams cheered. Their bristle-bot had scooted for a few inches before it died. But it had worked.

Maven looked at the materials in front of her. How were they supposed to make *that* from *this*?

"We should've watched them make it and then try

to imitate their steps," she said with regret.

Dominic scoffed. "What? And let them beat us?"

Maven braced herself against the edge of the desk and, looking at him, said, "This isn't the competition, Dominic. It doesn't matter if they build their model first. We're not being graded on this little bristlebot. But if we don't figure out how to do it ourselves, how can we teach our class?"

Dominic groaned and leaned back on his chair, balancing it on the two back legs. The motion made Maven a little dizzy.

"Okay, here it says to attach the little motor—that panel there—to the top of the cut-up brush. . . ."

Maven did as he read from the instructions.

The other pair of boys got theirs to work. It didn't stop after a few inches. It kept going until it drove over the edge of the desk and one of the boys caught it in his hands, stopping it from plunging to the ground.

"Easy!" he said, shooting a glance at Maven and Dominic, who were just getting started assembling their bot.

Even though she tried to block the jeers and taunts

from the other boys, Dominic's attitude was the hardest to ignore.

She put down the brush head and the motor and asked, "Why are you really so mad at me? It's not like I asked Mrs. Wagner for you to be my . . . co-leader."

"Assistant," Dominic pretty much spat the word. He shrugged. "It doesn't matter. I was punished for speaking up and saying what everyone else was thinking but was afraid to say."

"And what was that?"

His eyes flashed at her. "Will you cry if I tell you? If you end up crying, you can't blame me."

Maven clenched her teeth. "Tell me."

It was better to know the truth.

"This isn't your thing, Ortiz."

"I can learn. You don't know anything about robotics either."

"But do you play video games like Jane? Or do you know how to be friends with the boys like Gemma? No. You just want to do it all yourself, even when you aren't the right person to be the leader. You only know how to make up stories and boss people around.

You're like a mini teacher. Not cool, Ortiz. Not cool."

"You know nothing about me," she said, shaking with anger.

Dominic must not have expected this reaction from her because he opened his mouth to add, "I . . . it's just. It would've been easier if Reyker hadn't moved away. He's a coding genius."

"Too bad you only got me," Maven said, more determined than ever to prove Dominic wrong.

Before Dominic could fight back, Mrs. Callahan said it was time to get back to class. Maven collected her materials in seething silence while Dominic talked to the other student pairs. They had made their bristle-bots work and were saying how easy it would be to teach their classes how to assemble them.

Dominic sent her a loaded look, and although in another circumstance her first impulse would be to apologize, now she stared back at him until he was the one to avert his gaze.

Still, it didn't feel like a victory. She and Dominic were on the same team. But if they failed, the loss would look way worse on her than him. It wasn't fair.

She headed back to class.

"Good luck," Mrs. Callahan said.

Luck was something that no one could control. It wasn't smart to depend on it, but Maven appreciated the sentiment. "Thank you," she said, and left.

Later, when the final bell rang, Maven was relieved the week had finally come to an end.

Sylvie called out, "Maven! Wait up!"

Maven was already by the classroom door, but she halted to see what Sylvie needed. She hoisted her backpack higher on her shoulder. It was extra heavy with the robotics books she hadn't been able to read during lunch and recess anyway. After the fiasco with Dominic, she had a hard time concentrating on anything else. She felt like a swarm of scary wasps were buzzing inside her head.

"What's up?" Maven said, surprised that her voice sounded so distant.

"Hey, I had an idea," Sylvie said.

Maven's mind was still on the bristlebot fiasco, but she looked into the new girl's eyes and smiled back, making an effort to tune out the voices of the whole class celebrating the end of the first week back to class. But it was so hard.

"Do you want to go watch a movie tonight?" Sylvie asked brightly.

At first, Maven got excited. A movie night sounded fantastic.

But before she replied that she would love to, the backpack slipped off her shoulder again. The bristlebot kit didn't add that much weight, but it was the last drop that made the cup overflow, or the last straw that broke the camel's back. Or in this case, the last tiny thing that was about to break Maven's shoulder. She hissed in frustration as she hitched it up on her other side.

She needed to go home and figure out the silly bristlebot. If the other boys had managed to assemble it, it couldn't be that hard!

"Sorry," Maven said. "I've had a lot on my mind lately. What were you saying?"

"No biggie," Sylvie said, her smile fading. "I can just go to the movies with my brother if you can't."

Maven placed a hand on her new friend's shoulder. "I'd love to come along. It's just that I wanted to finish something today so I can enjoy the weekend. What about tomorrow?"

People were filing out of the class, skirting the girls who stepped away from the doorway they were blocking.

"I can't. We're visiting my grandma for her eightieth birthday this weekend."

"Oh, fun," Maven said, her heart sinking. She didn't want to say no to Sylvie. But at the same time, Maven knew she wouldn't be good company if she was preoccupied with the bristlebot.

"I'm going to try to finish as fast as I can, and then I'll call you," she said, although Sylvie looked like a deflated balloon. "Deal?"

Sylvie perked up a little. "Deal. Call me as soon as you finish. Bye!"

"Bye!" Maven said, waving enthusiastically.

But once she was home, she couldn't get to work right away. All week long, she had neglected her chores, and Papi was adamant she finish putting her laundry away before it got all mixed with the weekend load. Then the triplets arrived, and she had to sequester herself in her room so she wouldn't get distracted.

For all she tried though, she couldn't make the

bristlebot work. Maybe she got a bad one. Maybe the batteries were bad.

Maven never gave up, but she knew only too well that when a project got stuck, it was best to take a break.

She found Sylvie's mom's number and headed to the kitchen to ask her dad permission to go to the movies. She had to whisper so the triplets wouldn't overhear her. If they did, they'd want to come along, and at the moment they were perfectly entertained watching a fun show about puffins.

"What are you going to watch?" Papi asked while he made a batch of his famous kettle corn.

Maven's stomach growled with hunger. She shrugged. "I'm not sure," she said. "I didn't ask. Where's Gabriel, by the way?"

Papi smiled. "Oh, a little earlier today, I drove him to his friend's birthday party at the arcade. He'll be back in a couple of hours."

"Nice," Maven said. Her little brother had a more active social life than she did.

She dialed the number Sylvie had given her, and when a woman answered, Maven's heart raced, but she fought the urge to hang up.

"Hi, this is Maven. I'm Sylvie's friend from school."

"Hello, Maven," the woman said. By the background sound, Maven guessed she was driving. "I'm her mom. Sylvie told me about you. Thanks for inviting her to Girl Scouts! She loved it."

"Oh, nice!" Maven said, feeling especially proud of herself.

Maven hesitated a little at the pause that followed and then said, "It's just that Sylvie invited me to the movies, but I had something to finish at home. I told her I'd call her as soon as I was done. Is she still around?"

"I'm so sorry, but I just dropped her off at the theater with some new friends from the block just a few minutes ago. She'll be so sad she missed you."

"That's okay," Maven said, glad no one could see how her face flushed. "I'll see her at school on Monday. Have a good weekend!" she added, making sure her voice sounded extra cheerful even though she felt like crying.

"You as well. Bye!"

Maven hung up and stood in the kitchen, wishing

she could turn back time. This had been a terrible first week of school.

"Come sit with us!" Ruby called from the couch.

"Yes, come sit with us, Mavy," Grey and Valentina chimed in.

Papi must have overheard the conversation, or at least guessed what had happened, because he offered Maven a bowl of steaming popcorn and added extra chocolate chips, her favorite.

Maven sat next to her cousins, but she couldn't focus on the puffins, even if they were adorable.

She shouldn't have taken so long to decide to take a break. She should've accepted Sylvie's invitation at school. This was the first Friday night of fifth grade and she was spending it with her little cousins watching cartoons at home.

Not cool at all.

Chapter Ten

After struggling with it all weekend, Maven still didn't have success with the bristlebot.

On Sunday night, Tía Janette stopped by. She found Maven sitting at the table, staring at the mess in front of her.

"Oh, hi, Tía," Maven said when she realized her aunt had said hi.

"What's wrong, Mavencita?" Tía said, brushing Maven's hair lovingly. "Why do you look so sad?"

Maven shrugged. "I'm not sad. I'm just . . . frustrated."

Tía Janette sat next to her. "Why? What's wrong?"

"It's just that I can't get this thing to work," she said, motioning at the bristlebot parts scattered in front of her. "I'm following all the directions, but nothing I do matters."

Tía Janette glanced at the clock on the wall and asked, "Do you want me to help you figure it out?"

Maven hesitated. She too looked at the clock. It was very late. She was so tired she was seeing double. Finally, she nodded. "Okay. Thank you, Tía."

Tía Janette glanced at the instructions. which at this point Maven had memorized but still didn't understand. "Oh! I think you attached these parts upside down," Tía Janette said.

"Huh," Maven said, flipping the pieces and reattaching them right side up.

"And then," she said, biting her lip in concentration, "you hook these little cables by color with the switch off."

Maven scrunched her face in confusion. She was sure she had tried that. But she matched the colors again and moved the tiny switch on top of the bot. To her surprise, the bot's light came on!

"What? I did that like ten times!" Maven exclaimed, jumping to her feet.

Tía Janette smiled, satisfied. "Maybe it was my luck, then."

In that moment, Maven's dad walked in the kitchen. When he saw the bot wheeling over the table, he smiled. "You got it to work, Mav? Hurray!"

Maven winced. "Well, Tía helped me a little. A lot."

"You almost had it!" Tía said, patting Maven's hand. "I'm sure one more try, you'd have done it all on your own."

Maven was so delighted watching the little brush zooming over the countertop, but she was exhausted from working on it all weekend. She was so happy to finally go to bed.

The next day though, she had a slight headache. Dominic looked fresh as lettuce.

To Maven's relief, Sylvie looked like her happy, pleasant self.

"Sorry about Friday," she said. "I feel bad we left, but it was the last showing."

"Don't feel bad about it!" Maven said, perking up. "I should've called you as soon as I arrived home."

"Oh well," Sylvie said, opening her notebook for language arts. "What did you do anyway?"

Maven had hoped to avoid this conversation, but, trying to sound all casual, she said, "I just hung out with my cousins. They're triplets."

"Nice!" Sylvie exclaimed. "Do they go to this school?"

Maven ducked. "Nope."

"Are they in high school already?" Sylvie's eyes were shiny with curiosity.

"They're actually four years old," Maven said, trying to think of a cute story about them to share with her friend.

But Sylvie's reaction was very different from what Maven had prepared for.

"Oh no!" she said. "I'm sorry you were stuck babysitting. That sounds terrible."

Maven couldn't correct her because Mrs. Wagner asked the class to get to work. But she thought about Sylvie's words for a long time, and the more she did, the worse she felt about herself.

Finally, midmorning, Mrs. Wagner said, "Before our class representatives, Maven and Dominic, help us put together our first robot, let's go over some facts that will hopefully get you all interested in this new unit."

Some people had groaned in frustration. Maven

wished she could join the chorus. But she had to lead by example, so she kept her face blank. Or as much as she could.

"What makes a robot a robot?" Mrs. Wagner asked the class.

Zahara raised her hand. "It's a machine that performs automated tasks for which it was programmed."

"Excellent! Robots are used for many reasons. When I was a kid like you all, I thought that by now the world would be overpopulated by robots."

Christopher, one of Dominic's friends, laughed. "That hasn't happened yet!"

"Are you sure?"

Silence fell on the class as realization dawned on them. Robots were all around them. Maven had already reached this conclusion after her conversation with Jonah at the library.

"Tell me some examples of robots." Their teacher gave them a little time to think. "I gave you all a clue the other day when I mentioned my favorite vacuum cleaner."

It was as if a light had come on in the room. A bunch of hands went up.

"Self-driving cars."

"Rockets."

"Rovers in space," Zahara said.

"Robotic body parts," Sylvie added. "My grandpa has a bionic arm."

Maven looked at her with surprise. She hadn't known this about her new friend. Well, there were a lot of things she didn't know about Sylvie.

"Excellent answers, everyone!" Mrs. Wagner said. She turned toward the whiteboard and wrote four big letter *D*s.

Maven had seen the four *D*s in one of the articles that she had read, but everything was blending in her mind. She didn't remember what they stood for.

Mrs. Wagner turned toward the class and said, "Robots are used in many situations that can be described with any of these words: *dirty, dull, dangerous, dear.*"

"What's dull?" Jane asked. "Like, not sharp?"

"It can also mean boring. Tedious. A task so repetitive that it's better to have a machine do that job because they can do it faster and more efficiently than a person."

"Oh!" Dominic exclaimed, surprising not only Mrs.

Wagner but also Maven. It was the first time he'd acted even the tiniest bit interested in the topic. "Like the machine at the soda plant in Atlanta that puts the lids on the bottles."

"Perfect!" said their teacher. "Line work at a factory is one thing that robots are perfect for because a machine can do it without making a mistake or falling asleep at the job."

A buzz went over the classroom.

"Now, what about dirty?"

"A spill in the ocean or the river?" Sawyer said before Maven could answer.

"Bingo!" their teacher cheered. Her enthusiasm was contagious. "When it's a job like going into the sewers to fix a line or cleaning the floors like an automatic vacuum cleaner! If you really think about it, the little bristlebot we'll make later is just a very simple form of a linear-motion robot combined with one that senses obstacles. Linear motion means—"

"That it moves in a straight line," said Dominic.

"Excellent," Mrs. Wagner said. "Now, what about dangerous?"

"A rover on Mars!" Zahara said again.

"Or a submarine that can dive super deep," Sawyer added.

"Excellent! In those situations, some people also use a fifth *D*, which stands for *distant*. It can also mean that a place is too difficult for a human to reach, like the inside of your stomach, and so a doctor can send a tiny camera and robot to operate on people," Mrs. Wagner said. "Firefighters use robots when the situation is too dangerous for a person to assess. What about *dear*? What does *dear* mean in this context?"

Now everyone was silent as they tried to think.

"Expensive?" said Maven. Since Dominic had added to the conversation, why couldn't she?

"Good thinking," Mrs. Wagner said, and all of Maven felt like she was on fire, pleased with the compliment. "When sending people is too expensive, a robot is a good solution."

"Some situations are a combination, right?" Mimi asked.

Their teacher nodded. "And sometimes, some robots are created just to entertain. Can you think of robots you have around your house that fit this description?"

"I have a cat robot I got for Christmas because my

sister's allergic to real cats!" Claire said. "Her name is Misty. She evens purrs. She's purr-fect!"

The class laughed.

"I have a robot that follows me around and tells me jokes," said Ben.

"Is that why your jokes aren't even that funny?" his friend Logan teased him. "Maybe you need to re-program it."

"We have robots at school, believe it or not," Mrs. Wagner continued, trying to stop the boys from start-ing an argument.

"The student card scanner at the cafeteria," Maven exclaimed. She wasn't going to let this opportunity pass.

"Excellent, Maven! Good thinking!"

Maven exhaled with relief that she was able to put in a word during the discussion, but Ben and Logan were still arguing.

Mrs. Wagner clapped her hands to call for silence. "We have a robot in the media center that isn't very glamorous but keeps the fish alive."

"The fish tank cleaner!" Dominic exclaimed.

"That's right," said Mrs. Wagner.

"Wow," said Sawyer. "I never saw it that way."

"So today we'll put together this simple bristlebot. Who knows, tomorrow one of you can be the head of a project that builds a robot that knows exactly what you want to eat for dinner and shops, prepares, cooks, and cleans. All with the touch of a button."

There was a buzz of excitement in the room as Mrs. Wagner handed out the little boxes with the models to put together.

"I'm sure a lot of you have way more experience with robots than you think," she said. "Now, our leaders will help us assemble this tiny robot. Ready?"

She looked at Maven and Dominic and smiled, but neither one seemed ready, really. Maven wished with all her heart that she could just be a contributor instead of someone in charge.

But it was too late for that.

Besides, she had read a lot of things over the weekend, and she'd also learned a lot of new things during this lesson. She reminded herself she had signed the STEAM pledge and that she couldn't let the girls down. Most important, she wouldn't let Dominic think she wasn't up to the task just for being a girl.

"Ready," she said, and stepped forward.

Chapter Eleven

"You have to make sure you click the switch to off before you connect the cables," Maven said, trying to remember everything Tía Janette had explained to her. "Otherwise, if you connect them when the switch is on, it won't work." She smiled nervously. "I kept doing that for hours until my aunt showed me how."

She glanced at Mrs. Wagner, who nodded in approval. Dominic's eyes widened as if he hadn't known this.

Interesting.

Maybe he and Maven had been stuck on the same problem.

The class set out to build the model.

To everyone's surprise, Sylvie was the first person

who succeeded in assembling her bristlebot kit. Not only that, but soon after, the little funny bot was zooming all over the room. The boys scrambled to finish at least one among their group to catch up to the girls.

Dominic sent Maven a venomous look like it was her fault that the girls were winning. She had only volunteered to lead the project, and now this battle was her fault?

Mrs. Wagner must have sensed the tension because she turned on her tiny microphone clipped to the lapel of her jacket and announced, "Kids! It's not a competition among ourselves! A victory for one is a victory for all."

There was a lot of unhappy mumbling, and not only from the boys.

"Now we actually beat them at something, they want to take this away from us?" Claire complained.

She had a point.

Maven patted Sylvie's shoulder and said, "That was impressive. How did you do it?"

Sylvie, pink-cheeked and shiny-eyed, replied, "I just followed the instructions. But maybe I also got lucky and got one of the only working kits? I mean,

Zahara has retraced her steps three times. There's nothing wrong with how she put it together, except that hers doesn't work."

It wasn't that Sylvie was being falsely modest and trying to make others feel better about not getting their bots to work. What she said made sense.

"Okay, class, let's finish your kits at home so we can go over a few important things," Mrs. Wagner said.

Most people put away their kits, but Maven saw Zahara still working on hers behind a book she'd propped on the desk as if the teacher wouldn't notice. Mrs. Wagner must have been too tired to call her out because she kept on explaining how the word *robot* came from an old Slavic word that meant "drudgery" or "servitude." That different types of robots had different functions. "A robot needs to sense, compute, and act. We tend to think of robots only as androids, which means a machine that looks like a human. But like we talked about, a robot can even look like a cat or an everyday object. Now, we need to decide if we're going to build a robot that moves linearly like this little bristlebot—or one that performs a repetitive action."

"A vacuum!" Sadie exclaimed.

"A motion light!" Sawyer countered.

"What about a robot that detects offsides in soccer?" Logan asked.

From that, there was no compromise. A bunch of the girls played soccer, but if they voted with the boys, that would destroy friendship alliances left and right.

Mrs. Wagner, probably sensing that they would reach no consensus that day, said, "Think about your options. Next Monday, everyone will turn in a brief essay justifying their choice. And not only that, but I also expect everyone to give an idea of what materials we'd need to build the robot."

Despite her efforts to unify the class by dissolving the two rock-solid groups, by the time the lunch bell rang, everyone was mad at everyone else.

School had become the most stressful thing in Maven's life.

Maven couldn't distract herself from how much her life had changed since she'd volunteered to lead the competition. Even Sylvie and Zahara's conversation about the space rover Orion couldn't pull her in—and she'd spent an hour reading about it over the weekend. Mrs. Wagner had envisioned this as an opportunity to be more united as a class than ever.

But the opposite was true.

Maven scratched her head, worried that by the time they had to present their project, their class would be more divided than ever.

Chapter Twelve

With school being so stressful, Maven lived for Tuesdays.

Tuesdays meant Girl Scouts and Gemma. And this Tuesday, it meant a trip to the aquarium! Just what she needed.

She and Sylvie were the last to arrive at the library. They rode in the car with Vanessa while Gemma was in the car with Maggie. There were four other girls who grabbed the best spots (shotgun and the second row). Sylvie and Maven sat in the back, which was so narrow even Maven's short legs felt cramped, and she was by far the smallest of the group.

Vanessa had electronic dance music playing, but that made conversation impossible for Maven and

Sylvie to hear from the back row. Sylvie leaned forward between Sammy and Lola. Grace in turn leaned toward the front seat to chat with Thalia and Vanessa. Those girls attended a different school, and Maven liked them but didn't really know them as well as they knew each other.

At first, she felt left out, but then, she started enjoying the break from having to be *on* for other people. Maven let her thoughts wander.

Looking out the car window, she noticed a small robot delivering food and an animatronic panda at a car dealer waving at people. Even the traffic lights were technically robots. Robots were everywhere!

Maven was fascinated, but as they arrived at the aquarium, she was more than ready to enjoy time with real people.

Maggie had arrived first, and the first one to get out was of course Gemma, who ran in the direction of Vanessa's car. Maven smiled seeing the happiness on her friend's face to see—

"Sylvie!" Gemma exclaimed, picking Sylvie up a few inches from the ground, exuberantly.

Maven's stomach dropped to her feet.

"Mavy!" Gemma exclaimed too, and tried to pick up Maven. But maybe because Maven had been so afraid of falling, she'd planted her feet firmly to the ground and she and Gemma almost toppled to the side.

"I missed you!" Gemma said, looking at Maven like she hadn't seen her in forever. "Where have you been?"

But before Maven could reply, the other girls who had ridden with Vanessa had gathered around Gemma to say hi, and they whisked her away to make a funny video for social media.

"Let's go, Maven," Maggie called.

The rest of the troop was already lining up to go into the aquarium. The leaders assigned pairs so everyone could be safe and gave each girl a ticket.

"I'm so glad I got you!" Sylvie said to Gemma, and the girls briefly hugged.

Maven was the opposite of glad, but she still smiled at her buddy, Lola, who was heading toward Maven but glancing at Grace.

Vanessa said, "The aquarium is still fairly small, and those of you who've been here before will recognize some exhibits that survived the renovation. But there are a few new interactive activities that I think you will all love. Feel free to explore for . . ." She gazed at her watch for a few seconds, her forehead wrinkling in concentration as she calculated the time.

"Forty-five minutes," Maggie added, and the leaders laughed. They complemented each other perfectly.

"Right!" said Vanessa. "Explore for forty-five minutes, and then let's meet at the auditorium for the presentation. At next week's meeting, we'll talk about what we learned and do an activity."

"Sounds like a plan," Maggie said.

The girls rushed in after the leaders. Maven was last.

No one seemed to notice though. And maybe it didn't matter. But she was stressed, and it seemed that her feelings kept being hurt.

Maven had known most of these girls since kindergarten, and she was friends with all of them. But her number one was Gemma.

The only problem was that maybe for Gemma, Maven wasn't her number one anymore. Gemma and Sylvie walked around the exhibits arm in arm, talking and laughing about everything. Sylvie was new to the troop, not her. But she tried to tamp those feelings down and went around with Lola.

Lola too was quiet. More than usual. Maven wondered if she was bugged that she hadn't been paired up with Grace. The two were neighbors and close friends.

In any case, Maven followed her buddy.

The aquarium was so new it still smelled of fresh paint. There was even masking tape on a few baseboards, and a couple of exhibits had little "Coming Soon" signs. There was a platform that at first looked empty, but then when Maven walked up to the tank next to it, which held a family of turtles, a holographic figure shimmered in the air in front of her. Maven couldn't help smiling in delight.

It was the aquarium mascot, a mermaid with bronzed skin and long curly hair.

"Welcome to the aquarium! Home to so many species of fish, plants, and other creatures from the beautiful state of Georgia. My name is Savannah, and I'll tell you some fun facts about the rivers, wetlands, and other bodies of water around us."

"This is so cool!" Lola exclaimed next to Maven.

Soon, Maven and Lola were completely hooked

on the narration of the holographic mermaid that continued at each station and led to the next seamlessly, explaining facts about the different fish in the tanks that covered both walls of the hallway.

The presentation always ended on a cliffhanger. When the girls walked up to the next station, Savannah appeared and continued her narration. It seemed like magic, but Maven understood there must have been a motion sensor. She proved her point by going a few feet away and coming back and seeing the holographic mermaid appear and disappear. She was fascinated when she discovered that at the touch of a button, Savannah could switch to other languages, like Spanish, Vietnamese, Korean, French, and Yoruba! She also discovered that the speed of the mermaid's speech could be adjusted as well as the volume.

"Wow!" she gasped, when she saw live captions appear.

It would've been more fun to walk along with Gemma, but by the looks of it—actually, the sounds of it: loud laughter and shushing by the aquarium workers—Gemma and Sylvie weren't really paying attention to any of the presentations. They were just making the mermaid appear and then pause mid-sentence. The girls laughed at the hologram's frozen expressions.

Maven would've laughed at the funny face too, but she was annoyed that Gemma didn't even try to include her. Gemma didn't even look in Maven's direction. Secretly, Maven hoped they got called out.

In the meantime, she tried to concentrate on the school of catfish, and how even though rainbow and brown trout shared the tank, the two species kept to different areas. According to Savannah, catfish were bottom fishes and helped clean the tank. Maven also noticed a robot wiping the inside of the glass to keep it clear. In the back of the tank there was a panel showing the water temperature. And by the bubbles in one corner of the tank, she guessed the filters were hidden there behind aquatic plants.

There was a little fish swimming by itself, but seeing a group of other similar fish, it quickly swam in their direction. Maven smiled at how wanting to be part of the group seemed to be something fish and girls had in common.

By the end of a long hallway, Maven and Lola joined

Anika and Grace as they made their way through each exhibit. The four of them were chatting and laughing, but not like Gemma and Sylvie.

"I wonder what they're going to share at the meeting," Lola said, looking at Gemma and Sylvie over her shoulder. Her voice was definitely judgy.

Although Maven had been tossed aside like she didn't matter, and she was tempted to agree with Lola, she felt an obligation to her friends: the oldest one and the newest.

"That's just the way they are," Maven said. "They're not hurting anyone."

She didn't want to act like a goody-goody, and luckily Lola, Grace, and Anika didn't seem to take it that way because they didn't speak about Gemma and Sylvie anymore. Which was awesome, because a minute later, Gemma walked into the auditorium, looking around. When she caught sight of Maven, she grinned so wide Maven could see all the way to Gemma's capped back molars. Maven couldn't help but smile back.

Finally!

"Come sit with me!" Gemma said, waving over

Maven, who didn't waste a single second to join her.

"I have so much to tell you," Maven whispered right as the light was dimming before the 3D movie. School had been a nightmare, and she really wanted to talk to her friend.

But Gemma, in her rush to switch seats to leave room for Maven, hit her foot on something and yelped. Loudly.

Maggie turned around and looking at Maven said, "Girls, please. Remember we represent Girl Scouts. Best behavior, please."

"Oh," said Maven, her face burning with embarrassment.

Sylvie walked into the auditorium and sat on Gemma's other side. The two girls whispered loudly during the whole movie, even though Maggie kept looking back to see where the conversation was coming from. She looked at Maven, but Maven just looked ahead at the screen, hoping the 3D glasses were enough to cover the tears in her eyes.

Chapter Thirteen

In the end, there was no time to catch up with Gemma. It was all Sylvie's fault. Maven wished she'd never invited her to join Girl Scouts, that she'd never introduced her to Gemma. Maven had a hard time getting over it at school. Perhaps Sylvie guessed something was going on because even though they had lunch together, they barely talked.

Maven tried to do her schoolwork, but her mind kept wandering to the aquarium and Sylvie and Gemma laughing. Without her. The more and more she fixated on how Maggie had pointedly looked at Maven as if she had been the one not paying attention to the presentation, the more upset she became. She shook her head as if that gesture could shake off the intrusive thoughts.

. She was trying to come up with an idea for a robot, but her mind wasn't cooperating. If she couldn't even start with that, then she couldn't write the essay. And because she was the leader, her idea had to be the best. Once again, she went to sleep frustrated.

On Saturday, she remembered that among the Halloween decorations there had been a mechanical spider. If Maven could figure out how it worked, maybe she could try to duplicate the overall idea to make a butterfly or a firefly!

She found the box, but the spider had been taken apart, perhaps so it could fit in the box. Happily, Maven brought it to her room, and in a few minutes, she was able to put all the pieces together.

But, of course, when she turned the switch to the on position, the spider didn't move.

"Maybe the batteries are dead," she said, and was glad to find extra batteries in the kitchen cupboard.

Still, the spider was dead.

Stubbornly, she tried to find out online what was

wrong. At least she wasn't alone; Lucho snored at her feet.

It was the middle of the day, but if she opened the window and saw the glorious sunshine and heard the voices of the neighborhood kids playing, she'd never finish her assignment. So she'd closed the windows and put her mom's noise-canceling headphones on. If only there were a mute button in her mind that would quiet the scaries forever. They'd grown so much by now that she was thinking of naming them individually.

The little monsters. They were practically becoming tangible.

Like she always did, Maven followed the thought process into a monster rabbit hole, imagining the backstories of her scaries.

Great. Now they were *hers*.

The images of little creatures with fangs and claws was so vivid, she got goose bumps. She eyed the electronic spider with growing fear.

That's why she screamed and jumped from her chair when something touched her arm. Lucho jumped up and started barking at the intruder. But then he realized who it was and whined as if he were saying sorry.

It was Valentina, poor thing. The room was dark, but the expression of fear on her face was noticeable enough.

"Sorry, Valen!" Maven quickly said, trying to comfort her cousin. "I didn't mean to scare you, but you startled me, pumpkin!"

At the endearment, the little girl planted her feet solidly on the ground and squared her shoulders like she was about to get in a fight.

She narrowed her eyes at Maven and asked, "Are you a mountain troll that's pretending to be my cousin? She never calls me pumpkin." She tried to flip the light switch on, but she couldn't reach. So Maven turned on the desk lamp.

"Much better!" Valentina exclaimed.

Maven laughed but when she caught a glimpse of herself in the mirror across the room, she winced. Yikes! Valentina had a point.

Maven's hair was sticking out in all directions. She'd been so stressed, she'd mussed her hair, making it bigger and bigger by the minute. Her eyes were a little bloodshot from staring at the screen for so long, and her lips were dry. She hadn't had lunch, and now that she thought about it, she hadn't even had a sip of water since the early morning. She must be dehydrated.

"I'm sorry," she said in a sweet voice. She opened the blackout curtains and made an effort not to back away from the bright sunshine in case Valen accused her of being a vampire next. "It's me. Same old Maven . . ."

"What are you doing, Maven, and why don't you have time to play with us or tell us stories? You're even keeping Lucho in here," Valen said with a pout. She knew how to get to Maven's heart.

Maven sighed and sat on the floor, wishing she could speed up time and just have the competition be over with.

"I just can't figure it out," she said, glancing at the electronic spider on her desk.

"What is it, Mavy? Maybe we can help?" Gabriel asked. Grey and Ruby, who were standing behind him in the hallway, nodded. Maven was about to explain when a rustling sound interrupted her.

The robot spider that she'd been trying to assemble and failed to do so for the last couple of hours moved! First a leg twitched, and then the other.

Valentina's scream pierced through Maven's initial

delight that her efforts hadn't been in vain after all. Valentina's piercing scream turned into a wail when the robotic spider fell off the desk and made a beeline toward the door. Where the kids were standing.

At first, Gabriel laughed, but Valentina's fear was contagious.

"No!" Ruby screamed, putting herself in front of her sister. Gabriel tried to pick up Valentina, who was also trying to climb into his arms.

Maven didn't know which way to run.

The most surprising reaction was Grey's though. Shy, careful, gentle Grey, believing that his sisters and cousins were being attacked by a giant hairy spider grabbed the umbrella from the stand next to Maven's door and smacked the robot without a second thought.

"Don't! Wait! You're going to break it!" Maven yelled.

But Grey was on a mission. "Take that, you monster! Leave us alone!" As he hit the robot, the motor started whirring louder and louder until it stopped.

The silence was deafening.

The proud look on Grey's face was something to behold.

"Oh no!" Maven exclaimed, devastated as she moved the umbrella that was all broken and the smashed spider underneath the spokes.

Maven plopped to the ground, too tired to react.

"Is it dead?" Valentina asked, tears streaking down her face.

"Maven?" asked Grey. "I pwomise I didn't hit her!"

"Not Maven!" Gabriel said, laughter in his voice although he looked scared too. "The thing? What was it?"

Maven sighed. "The thing is certainly dead," she said. "But it was never really alive."

"Was it a zombie?" Ruby asked, hiding her face with her pudgy little hands.

Maven didn't want to laugh, but if she didn't, she was going to cry.

"It was a mechanical spider. I was studying it to make a similar robot for the robotics competition," she said.

"Oh, Mavy," Valen said. "I'm sorry!" Her lower lip started quivering. And then Ruby started sniffling.

"You mean I didn't save you?" Grey asked with a little voice.

Gabriel and Maven exchanged a panicked look.

The triplets were always intense and emotional. And after a full day of playing out in the sunshine, and the scare with the mechanical spider, their nerves were frayed. Adding to the fact that their active imaginations were fed by Maven's stories was the fear that their actions had somehow ruined Maven's hard work. It was all a formula for drama.

Their sadness had no end.

It had always been like this. Once one started crying, the others followed. There was nothing else to do but try to comfort them as their emotions ran out.

"Oh no," said Gabriel. "I better get Tía Janette. She had made lemonade and cupcakes and sent Valen to get you, and when she took so long, we came to see what had happened."

But Tía Janette was already there. Mami peeked behind her, her face sleepy and worried. Maven forgot her mom was still sleeping in preparation for tonight's shift.

But the worst was the look of sadness on the triplets and her brother as they stared at the ruined robot.

Chapter Fourteen

That night, her dad was reading a story to Gabriel. While he read to her brother, Maven did the dishes, her least favorite chore.

She wondered if there was a way to create a dish-washing robot, not just a machine that needed to be loaded and unloaded. But she put the idea aside. She couldn't make it happen, at least not in time to win the competition at the end of the term.

She just needed *one* good idea.

She remembered that once upon a time, she'd read that since the light bulb had been such a wonderful idea and had changed the world in unimaginable ways, it was now the ultimate symbol for a good idea.

She imagined that years and years in the future,

when people wanted the exact picture of someone un-inspired and in trouble, there would be *her* fifth-grade picture right next to it. Then she would be famous, but not cool. Her stomach churned again.

Now her hands were pruney beyond recognition and all the dishes were done. The sink and counter spotless. In her mind there wasn't even a firefly glow of an idea. Much less a light bulb!

In the background, Papi's voice went on and on as he read the story about two siblings engaged in an epic lemonade war. Maven tried to tune out the words. The last thing she needed was to get an idea for the wrong kind of project.

She dried her hands and sat down in front of the laptop one more time. Without letting herself stare at the screen in case the scaries took charge, she started typing nonsense.

I have no idea what I'm doing.

I'm a storyteller, not a scientist. Come on, light, turn on.

But soon, the words took a different direction. In the back of her mind, a little idea lit up, all from the memory of Valentina on her tiptoes trying to turn on the light and not reaching the switch.

Maven's mind was fuzzy at first, but there was definitely something there. She wanted to create something that helped people, that made life easier. But just when it seemed she was about to catch her big idea, it fluttered away.

She wasn't going to give up though. After all, she was responsible for her class.

Nothing that was worth it was ever easy, right?

She imagined how in the future Mrs. Wagner would brag to her class about how Maven's idea had been fabulous, but she didn't know how to make that fantasy come true. She hoped that next time a girl volunteered to lead the robotics project, the boys in her class wouldn't laugh like the boys in hers had. She wanted to be known for something important.

As she typed and typed, the idea glowed brighter. The image came up sharper. She got so carried away writing about a robot that could turn the light on for someone who couldn't reach the light switch (genius!).

Next, she borrowed Gabriel's markers and crayons and started on the design. She put her paper up and stared at it proudly. Her drawing skills needed a lot of work, but her assignment was finished, right as the clock marked her bedtime.

"A smiling Maven?" her dad said in a whisper as he walked in the kitchen. "That's my favorite kind of Maven."

She returned the smile but put the paper down, self-conscious.

Her dad ruffled her hair. "What's the matter, sweetheart?"

His dark brown eyes were pools of understanding. As a librarian, it wasn't that he knew the answer to every question or problem, but he knew where to find those answers. Perhaps . . . perhaps he could help her?

"I have to turn in an essay about a robot, why it's necessary, and what kind of materials I would need to build it," she said. "I've been trying all weekend, but my mind was blank, Papi. Has that ever happened to you?"

He nodded, his lips pressed. "More times than I can count. But I see you managed to get something written. How did you do it?"

She grinned sheepishly. "Butt in chair, like you always say. And once I got going, the idea kept growing. I thought about a mechanical arm that can extend high enough to flip a light switch for someone who can't quite reach, you know?"

His eyes lit up as he read. "This is great." He glanced at the rustic sketch on her paper. "I like your imagination, Maven!"

She squirmed uncomfortably. Being praised for her imagination wasn't what she had been aiming for.

In robotics and science in general, one needed to be all scientific and data driven. She'd been so proud at her progress. But now that she really looked at her work, the essay didn't look or sound like the scientific papers online. And her diagram was cute when she'd been going for utilitarian and precise.

The little vine-like design she'd added to the margin was decorative and unnecessary.

"I can't help myself," she said with a disappointed sigh. "I get carried away. I guess my imagination is out of control."

She felt like crying.

"Come here, Mavencita," Papi said, drawing her into his arms. "You actually think that science and imagination are opposite ends of the spectrum, don't you?"

She pulled back to look into his eyes and asked, "But they are, aren't they? Science is all measurements and numbers and formulas. I can't design a robot, Papi, much less write the code to program it. I can make a drawing of what I think it can look like. And even if this is a good idea, how am I going to make it work? I can build it out of foam noodles, but how do I make the structure move?"

Her dad smiled. "Even in robotics, the design— the actual building and the coding—isn't done by the same person, love." He shook his head and continued, "And going back to my point about creativity—which is another word for *imagination*—and science, they go hand in hand. If it weren't for the daydreamers of the world, we wouldn't even have found a way to use fire. The what-ifs are what makes the mind leap into realities that a generation ago seemed like science fiction. My phone for example—"

"I know," she said with a smile. "Your phone replaced a camera, camcorder, calculator, ATM, et cetera, et cetera, et cetera. The teacher told us that last week."

"Because we're from the same generation that saw a small idea give way to many more, and now here we are. Look around us: microwave, dishwasher, clothes washer, the toaster even. It knows what to do and does it. Machines and robots are amazing, but they're only possible because someone had an idea, and maybe someone else improved it, and then another person built and implemented it. And someone else fixed the glitches, and on and on. See?"

She could see what he meant. And for the first time, she understood that even if her mind was more artistically oriented, she could use her imagination to not only have a good idea but also to lead her class.

But it was the night after an intense weekend, and she was tired. Her brain was fried. She yawned.

Her dad kissed her forehead and said, "Time for bed."

"I need to print the report first," she said.

He grimaced. "We can print it out tomorrow."

His feud with the family printer was legendary. The printer worked without a hitch when Gabriel wanted to print out pictures to copy from the internet, but when the family needed it for something urgent (like, a field trip authorization, or copy of important documents, or the last grant Papi had written), it went haywire and Papi had to reprogram it. Every time.

"I'll get up a little early to make sure it works," he said, and although he didn't particularly say the word *promise* when he said he was going to do something, he did it.

"Thank you, Papi," she said, "Good night."

She marched into her room, and a sharp pain pierced her foot.

"Ouch!" she yelped.

"Are you okay?" Papi called from the kitchen.

Maven looked at the bottom of her foot, where a building block was still attached. She'd never stepped on one before, and now she knew firsthand how much it hurt. Papi's and Mami's complaints had been well-founded. Maybe she could invent a robot that would somehow detect stray blocks and pick them up before someone got hurt?

She didn't know how she'd go about bringing this to life, but like Papi had said, those details could be someone else's obsession.

She couldn't help it. She laughed. Now she couldn't stop thinking of robot ideas.

She placed the building block on her nightstand

and got into bed.

The scaries tried to remind her one more time how silly her idea was. How she was going to let her class down. But Papi's reminder that creativity and science could indeed go hand in hand was louder than the scaries.

So the scaries changed tactics. Since Maven ignored them when she was awake, they decided to tell her what they thought of her idea in a dream.

The kind of dream she hadn't had since she was a little girl.

Chapter Fifteen

Maven dreamed that she was up on Fairy Meadow. A swarm of flickering lights surrounded her, but she loved the tickling of soft gossamer wings on her skin. A tune like that from a music box rang in the Forest of Magicstan, and Maven twirled. Her long dress glittered like diamonds.

She caught one of the flying fairies on her hand carefully so she wouldn't hurt it and stared at the creature for a second.

When her eyes focused on the creature's face, her smile froze. The scaries in her mind screamed that the dream had taken a sharp turn into Nightmare Alley.

This wasn't a fairy. This was a giant fly!

She dropped it, and just like that, the magic ended.

All the flying fairies thudded to the ground. The scenery changed as if the backdrop had just been reflected by a projector that had been abruptly turned off.

An eerie silence filled her ears until they rang painfully.

"What's that sound?" she said aloud, although she was alone in a vast, empty, foggy space.

But a buzzing seemed to be coming from the ground where the fairies had dropped like black pebbles. She picked one up, and the pebble started vibrating in her hand. Only it wasn't a pebble anymore. It was a firefly made of teeny tiny plastic blocks. Maven studied it so carefully to understand how it was made so she could re-create it for her project that it fell off the edge of her open hand. In an instant, it assembled alongside the other fireflies on the ground. One piece clicking to the next and the next, until it formed . . .

A giant hand that looked just like Frankenstein's monster's hand. Before Maven could react, the green robotic hand picked Maven up by the back of her shirt and swung her in the air.

"Let me down!" she screamed.

The giant hand paused. Was it thinking? Was it

trying to obey her?

"Oh no," Maven said, noticing how far from the ground she was.

Before Maven could instruct it to gently place her on the ground, the hand loosened its grip and . . .

"No!" Maven said. "Don't drop me!"

The hand tightened again, but the fabric of her shirt ripped.

Maven fell.

She fell down,

down,

down, until she woke with a jolt in her bed.

She was safe. It was a dream. A nightmare. But it had seemed so real!

The building block was still on the nightstand, of course. In the daylight she noticed it was dark green.

She gasped, struggling for breath, but relieved that it had all been the product of her anxious imagination. And then, the proverbial light bulb went on in her mind.

She knew how she would bring her robotics project to life so her class would win the competition. She'd then go on and become the greatest robot builder in the history of robotics.

But first things first. She'd borrow Gabriel's blocks and somehow animate, or code them, or whatever it was called when something comes to life like Frankenstein's monster.

What had the scientist used? Electricity!

She didn't know how electricity worked, but she knew the electricity from a socket could be very dangerous. Even fatal.

Batteries! She'd use batteries to bring it to life!

"Gabi!" she called, flinging the covers aside. "I need something!"

A couple of moments later, a bleary-eyed Gabriel popped his head into her room. "What's wrong, Mave? I was having a good dream—"

"Gabriel! I need all the blocks you can find," she said, interrupting him before he got carried away. "I have an idea!"

Her wonderful mind had given her all the tools she needed to be successful. Now she needed only to follow the plan before the details vanished like the dreams usually do.

Gabi blinked and became alert immediately.

"On it!" he said and dashed to the playroom straightaway.

It seemed the whole family was eager for the robotics project to be done and over once and for all, too.

Chapter Sixteen

Maven walked into the classroom with her essay in hand, her face lit up with enthusiasm. She had built an arm made out of blocks but hadn't been able to bring it to life. No problem though. Maybe someone in the class could figure it out.

She had a feeling that today everything would go according to plan. The printer had worked without a hitch, and although the memory still made her heart speed up, her mind had given her the idea she'd been fishing for over the last few days. Finally.

But once she was sitting at her desk, her enthusiasm dimmed a little. Maybe she was just tired after a night f ull of nightmares and building furiously in the morning.

"Class," Mrs. Wagner called. "We'll start presenting

your ideas for a robot in desk order. Logan, you'll go first, and then the rest of your row, and so forth."

Maven, sitting at the middle desk on the left would go third to last.

At first, she was excited about the prospect of going at the end and blowing everyone's mind with the brilliance of her idea for a robotic arm that could switch the light on and off on command. But as Logan started presenting his idea for a remote-controlled car, she realized that going toward the end was the worst that could have happened to her. She was so nervous that sweat was dripping from her armpits. The sweat would definitely show in the fabric. She clamped her arms tightly to her body.

"And why do you think this robot is necessary?" Mrs. Wagner asked, taking notes on her clipboard.

"To have fun," Logan said proudly. "You said it's okay for some robots to be entertaining."

The boys of the class clapped as he took his seat, and Zahara went next.

Her idea was for a rover that could collect data from an inhospitable planet.

"The purpose is to give us information on how

humans can one day survive outside of Earth," she said, anticipating the teacher's question.

"Excellent!" Mrs. Wagner said as the girls clapped enthusiastically.

The score of the two unofficial groups in the class was even.

Boys one. Girls one.

There were presentations for a fish that cleaned the ocean, robotic dolphins that performed to amuse spectators so real dolphins didn't have to live in captivity, and robots that painted soda cans. Claire presented about a robotic pet walker that looked like one of those pony rides at festivals, and Ben showed designs of a robot that would throw basketballs to a player to dunk in the basket.

"I got the idea from the pitching machine at my little sister's softball practice," he said at the end of his presentation.

Claire chimed in, "I'm pretty sure that's already been invented . . ."

Ben looked like a raccoon caught in the headlights. Maven had seen one last summer, and the image was imprinted in her mind. She felt bad for Ben.

"Class," Mrs. Wagner intervened. "I'm sure most of you have realized that a lot of the ideas we're proposing are for things that have already been invented."

A rumbling of voices went over the class, echoing the whispering in Maven's mind.

"I love original ideas like Claire's pet walker, but let's not shoot down variations of things we already have in real life. An important part of innovation is using a tool for a different purpose from which it was intended," Mrs. Wagner said. "Now let's give Ben a round of applause for adapting the softball pitcher for basketball."

Ben looked a little more at ease. He sat right in front of Maven, which meant she was next. Her palms prickled with sweat. Even the scaries were so frightened they had no words to whisper into her ear.

When the clapping for Ben died down, she stood up and walked toward the front of the class. She placed her paper on the projector. Everyone was staring at her intently, but good thing no one laughed at how frilly her sketch was.

"I was inspired by my little cousins. They're triplets, you see?" she kept her eyes on Mrs. Wagner to distract herself from the snickers that had started in the back of the room. "They're too small to reach the light switch and—"

"Little cousins? That sounds more like herself, doesn't it?" It was definitely Logan's voice.

"Logan." Mrs. Wagner called him out. "When you presented, Maven and the rest of the class listened respectfully. Please, extend the same courtesy."

Logan winced. "Sorry, Maven," he mumbled.

Mrs. Wagner signaled to Maven that she should continue.

Maven cleared her throat. Her nose itched, but she didn't want to scratch in case she had sweat stains in her shirt. But the worst was that the script vanished from Maven's mind like the scenery had vanished in her dream. She had to improvise. Improvising was her least favorite thing to do, besides failing. She had no choice but to trudge on though.

She swallowed the knot in her throat and continued. "I was inspired by a crane that was cutting a tree in my neighbor's yard. The end of the mechanical arm had pincers, and the pincers in the other arm held the cut limb in place so it wouldn't fall on the house or someone." It was true, in a way. She had seen a crane cutting the neighbor's tree in the summer, but the idea had come to her in a dream. She didn't want to share that though, because it sounded so unscientific.

Their teacher nodded approvingly.

"In my design, which I confess, I don't know how to bring to life, a motion sensor will calculate the height of a short person and then will send a command to the tip of the arm to flip the switch that is out of reach," Maven said, and she shrugged.

"Brava, Maven! You're the first one who's mentioned thinking about bringing your project to life!"

Maven's cheeks warmed up, and she imagined she was blushing. She was too delighted to be embarrassed.

After the last presentations, Mrs. Wagner said, "I love that everyone's letting their imaginations fly! Not ruling out something just because it seems impossible or too simple means that you're leaving room for wonder! Wonder, curiosity, and ingenuity are the secret ingredients for big breakthroughs!"

Their teacher's enthusiasm was catching. Maven felt a buzzing in her ears, and she looked around in case her nightmare came true and little mechanical insects appeared to haunt her. But, of course, nothing of the sort happened.

"My dad says that necessity is the mother of ingenuity," Sylvie said.

"And my grandpa says that laziness is the cause of inventions," Christopher chimed. "He says that, back in his day, kids sharpened their pencils manually, and now we have electronic sharpeners. And not only that, he says that farmers used to plow the ground with oxen, and now there are machines that make perfect grooves for the seeds, and machines that harvest grain."

"My grandma told me how she used to stitch by hand and then machines took over. But now there's a revival of craftmanship and she gets paid a lot of money for handstitched clothes," Emilee added. "She has a boutique next to the Yellowstone park."

"Exactly," Mrs. Wagner said. "So we see that robots and machines automatized work to make things safer for humans. To help us have free time for other endeavors. A farmer who doesn't spend days plowing the ground, now can have time to study the market in which he will sell his product. Or a dairy owner can milk ten cows at once instead of spending all day doing it by hand."

"But some robots don't give you extra time," Dominic said, like always looking for ways to dampen the mood. "They make you waste time on, like, toys and stuff."

"But playing isn't a waste of time," Mrs. Wagner said. She looked at Maven, who was still standing at the front of the class. "You can sit down, Maven. Good job. Good job to all."

The class had been stressful because of the anticipation of waiting to present. But it had also been entertaining. Maven couldn't believe that it was almost lunch time.

Mrs. Wagner wasn't done yet, though.

"Now that we have all shared different ideas," she said, "let's break out into groups and discuss which ideas the class should plan, build, and code."

The class murmured as people tried to make sure they'd end up with their friends. Mrs. Wagner soon took control of the situation. "We'll gather in the same groups that did the research from the reading list Dominic and Maven shared at the beginning of the unit. This part requires leaving egos aside, okay? It was fun to just let our imaginations fly, but now we need to talk about the practical aspects of it."

Maven cleared her throat and raised her hand. "Mrs. Wagner, Dominic and I weren't in a group before."

Dominic nodded as he lowered his hand. He'd been about to ask the same question.

"You two can join Claire, Zahara, and Logan," she said.

"Bummer," Sylvie whispered.

Maven sent her a small smile. Ever since the incident at the aquarium, she'd been avoiding Sylvie. Now she felt a little guilty that she'd been happy not to be in the same group as her new friend.

Dominic didn't look happy with the group assignment though. His ears were bright red although his face was pale.

"But there's more girls than boys in that team, I mean, group."

The corner of Mrs. Wagner's mouth twitched. It seemed to Maven that she was trying not to roll her eyes. "That doesn't matter, Dominic! In fact, part of your grade will be showing the ability to get along with everybody. It is unacceptable to disrespect your classmates. I will not tolerate anyone treating someone badly because of their gender. Clear?" Their teacher was definitely losing her patience.

Dominic didn't reply, but Maven could tell he was clenching his teeth.

The class was a chaos of sounds for a few minutes as groups gathered to discuss their options.

"I think we can all agree that Maven's idea is great, but there's no way to bring it to life," said Claire.

Maven's words of protest vanished in her mouth before she could set them free. From the corner of her eye, she saw Mrs. Wagner following the discussion. Maven remembered that being a leader meant showing things by example. So although it was difficult, she nodded, and the group started analyzing the other options.

After some back-and-forth, Claire's idea of an automatic pet walker was the winner. At least in their little group.

Both Maven and Dominic looked crestfallen by the time the bell rang announcing lunch. They exchanged a look of solidarity that took Maven by surprise, but they walked on opposite sides of the hallway as they headed to the cafeteria.

Chapter Seventeen

At the end of the week, when Claire's idea of the pet walker had been voted to the final round along with Sawyer's idea of a temperature-checking robotic fish for aquariums, Maven was heading to the media center.

Honestly, she was still upset her idea of the robotic light switch was the first one to be chopped down by her group. But now she wanted to help Claire's idea win. She'd overheard Dominic promising Sawyer he'd vote for him even though Claire had been in his original group.

"Maven! Aren't you supposed to be heading to the bus?" Sylvie asked, pulling her out of her thoughts.

"Actually, I have to get something from the library,"

Maven said, picking at her nails.

"Oh!" Sylvie laughed. "You remind me of Gemma when she's zigzagging defenders."

Gemma! What was she up to? Maven missed her so much. She couldn't wait to see her bestie and forget about robots and technology.

"Gemma gets hyperfocused sometimes," Maven said, not loving the way Sylvie talked about Gemma as if they were best friends.

"She does! She asked me about you yesterday when we were at her house," Sylvie said, walking along with Maven. "She misses you."

Maven's scalp prickled, although her body had gone cold all over. "Yesterday?" she asked, although a bunch of questions had popped in her mind.

Sylvie nodded but didn't say anything more to explain why she'd been hanging out with Maven's best friend. And they hadn't even invited her!

"I was busy anyway," Maven said in a sharp voice that came out of nowhere.

It was obvious Sylvie sensed something had bothered Maven because after an uncomfortable moment, she shrugged and said, "Anyway, see you later."

Maven was still seething when she arrived at the media center. She walked in just as Dominic was leaving, his backpack fuller than usual. He smirked at her, but she tried to ignore him.

When the librarian told her the last book about the topic had just been checked out, Maven wished she'd said something to the one who was supposed to be her assistant.

"Now run to the bus before it leaves you behind," the librarian said.

Maven glanced at the clock and took off running. She was going to miss the bus!

Not only had Sylvie stolen her best friend, but she'd made her late to the library and Dominic had beat her to it, and now she was about to miss the bus.

All these thoughts flew out of her mind when she arrived at the bus stop and saw her little brother at the end of the line of kids. He had an odd, sad look on his face.

When Gabriel saw Maven, he smiled, but the smile didn't reach all the way to his eyes.

Maven wanted to ask what was bothering him, but the bus driver revved the engine. This was the last warning for everyone to get on before he closed the doors. Gabe got on the bus, and Maven followed. But as she walked to join her brother in the last double seat, she caught a glimpse of Sylvie's brother's car heading down the street. And the two girls in the back seat: Sylvie and Gemma.

"Finally," Gabriel said in a little voice next to her. "I need to tell you something."

Maven felt pulled in two directions.

One part of her wanted to be there for Gabriel, who obviously was going through something, and another one of course wanted to know why her friends were hanging out without her. But then she remembered that when Sylvie had asked her to go to the movies, she'd stayed home working on her project. . . .

"Maven," Gabriel said, shaking her arm. He'd obviously been talking, but she had no idea what he had said. He could tell, and his eyes filled with tears. "I asked you if you could read me a story when we get home."

The last thing Maven wanted to do once she arrived home was read a story. She wanted to be in her room by herself and figure out what was happening with her friend. But she didn't have the heart to say this to her brother.

"I have a lot of homework I need to catch up on." It was true. Because of the robotics project, she'd been neglecting her other subjects.

"You've been so busy lately. The triplets miss you. A lot," he said with an adorable pout.

Tenderness bloomed in Maven's heart. "Only the triplets?"

Gabriel shrugged. "Well, I miss you too. And I miss your stories!"

"Papi has one of those audiobooks from when he was young. I'm sure that if you ask nicely, he'll play it for you all. That way you can draw while the cassette tape reads to you."

"Okay," he said, not sounding too convinced.

To be honest, Maven missed him and the triplets too. She vowed to prepare something fun for the weekend. After a full summer of fun activities, she'd gone full MIA on them, and it was hard for the little ones to adapt.

Chapter Eighteen

When Maven was done with her homework, the triplets had already left. She felt bad she hadn't had time to even play a round of duck-duck-goose with them like Gabriel had begged her to.

Gabriel sat in the kitchen, coloring in his sketch pad. He hunched his shoulders when he saw her, and Maven could tell he was upset with her.

"Hi, Gabi," Maven said, ruffling his hair as she walked into the kitchen.

"Don't do that!" he complained.

Maven, whose heart was already tender for being left out of whatever Sylvie and Gemma's plans were, flinched.

"Okayyy," she said. "I see you're grumpy with me,

and I don't know why."

"Maybe ask yourself why, Maven," Gabriel said, his voice shaky.

"I don't know what you're talking about," she said, rolling her eyes, but she felt guilty all the same. Deep in her heart she knew she had hardly spent any time with him.

"Don't roll your eyes at me. You always do that, Mavy," he said, tears splashing his cheeks now.

"What's going on?" Mom asked, coming in from outside with a basket of laundry.

The scent of sunshine and clothes detergent was one of Maven's favorite smells ever, but now it failed to cheer her up.

"Mavy is being mean," Gabriel blurted out.

"Am not!" she exclaimed. She'd had a very tough few days that had turned into weeks, and she wished her brother understood that.

"Are too!"

"What? Gabe, I just tried to be playful with you, and you snapped at me!" she didn't intend to yell, but if the strain in her vocal cords was any indication, she just had.

Mami's shoulders sagged when she sighed like she was trying to defuse the situation by blowing at it. She placed the laundry basket on the table. Outside, it had started to rain.

Gabriel looked at Maven with brown eyes shimmering.

"Oh, Gabito," she whispered. "I'm—"

"No, I get it. You're all grown up and cool and don't have time for me anymore," he said, putting a hand out as if that could stop her apology. It was kind of cute, and kind of funny, but most of all, the gesture made her sad.

All her life she'd been proud to be the best older sister. She didn't understand why her friends complained about their little siblings so much. She always said it was easy to get along with Gabriel because he was adorable, her mini-me. But the truth was that secretly Maven was proud of the work she'd put into their relationship from the moment he'd come home and ended her reign as an only child. Of course they bickered once in a while, but they never really fought.

"Gabi," Maven said, wishing they could start all over, that they could turn back time and unsay the mean words and erase the annoyed gestures. But that's never possible. And the only way was through, as she well knew.

Gabriel softly closed his notebook and headed to his room. The click of his door hit her like a physical blow.

Dinner that night was quiet and uncomfortable. Mami and Papi exchanged worried looks but didn't ask Gabriel and Maven what the issue was. Gabriel pretended Maven didn't even exist, so she gave up trying to get him to talk to her.

But by the time she went to bed, Maven was almost in tears. Gabriel's words had pierced her heart. She'd been so determined to be cool for her friends at school, but her efforts hadn't succeeded. And now she had ruined her relationship with her brother and had hardly played with the triplets at all.

During their usual nighttime charla before Mom's shift, Maven finally poured her heart out.

"Mami," she said, looking at her mom with regret. "I know I had a bad mood when I walked in from school, and maybe my bad vibes were catching, but I think Gabriel also was dealing with something at school and he took it out on me. Did he say anything?"

"He had a fight with Rita, his best friend over a group project. And apparently, he's not cool enough because he doesn't have a phone," Mom said. She chuckled, but it was obvious she wasn't amused.

"They're in second grade!"

"I know . . ."

Maven stepped closer to her mom to help her fold the sheets and sneak in a good sniff of sunshine and soap. Outside, the rain kept falling and the sound was so comforting.

"What would they say about me, then?"

"What do you mean?"

Maven squinted her eyes at her mom and placed a hand on her waist. "Seriously? If being cool means having a phone in second grade, then I'm three years behind the coolness scale."

"Aw! Tough life!" Mom said, and ruffled Maven's hair.

Maven's parents had strict rules about phones.

Mom held a sheet close to her chest and said, "Are you really the only one without a phone, Maven? Is it that hard?"

Maven was tempted, just a teeny tiny bit, to say she

was the only kid in upper elementary just to see what her mom would say. But she could tell her mom really wanted to know if their rule was doing more harm than good. She couldn't lie, even if it was a white lie.

"Sylvie doesn't have one either," she said.

"Oh yeah. Sylvie. Is she the new girl?"

Maven noticed that her smile had turned into a frown when she thought of her new friend. "Yeah."

"Oh!" Mom said, her face lighting up with understanding. "I met her at Gemma's house—"

"What?" Maven asked a little sharper than she'd intended, but maybe her mom didn't think so, because she said, "Yes, she went to the movies with Gemma on Friday. I stopped by their house for a few minutes to drop off a book Rachel had requested from Papi's library and saw them together. Sylvie said you invited her to the troop meeting and she and Gemma clicked immediately. That's so nice of you, sweetheart. I'm so proud of what a good friend you are."

She already knew Gemma and Sylvie were hanging out together, and that they'd tried to include her, but it still hurt. She'd been too busy. So busy that she'd blown off her friends and never asked Gemma and Sylvie about their lives at all.

Maven felt that heavy lead ball in the pit of her stomach again rock from side to side as if the scaries were bowling.

Some friend she was! All this time she'd told herself that Sylvie had stolen her best friend and that Gemma had tossed her aside like she didn't matter.

But had they really?

Maven couldn't really blame her friends, old and new. She hadn't really been available to hang out since she'd been so busy dealing with Dominic being mean to her and all the work for the robotics project. More than project, obsession!

She'd made a mess of everything, and she felt more alone than ever.

Chapter Nineteen

The next morning dawned sunny and bright. Maven tried to capture a little bit of the brightness. True, the night before, when her mom had left for work, she'd stayed up worrying about how she'd ruined her friendship with Gemma and Sylvie. But now, she was determined to turn the page and make things right.

Things meaning the situation with her brother and with her friends, and the robotics project. They all seemed dire, but after a good night's sleep, she knew that she could only take one step at a time.

First on her list was making her peace with Gabriel. She knew from experience that she couldn't pretend nothing had happened with Gabriel. Her brother had been right. She'd left him aside for days, and when he'd needed a friendly, sisterly ear, she hadn't been there for him.

She wanted to make sure he knew she was on his side before they headed to school.

Apparently, Gabriel had been up for a while judging by the sounds of the audiobook coming from his room.

When the story ended, Maven knocked on her brother's room.

"It's open," Gabriel said.

Maven stopped at the door.

Gabriel looked so little sitting in front of his desk with his shoulders hunched. He held a blue pencil in his hand, but he wasn't coloring. He was just looking at the blank page as, once again, the tape played a story about fireflies.

Something clicked inside Maven.

He looked just like she felt. Lonely.

"Hey, Gabi," she whispered.

He turned around, and the look of relief and happiness on his face filled Maven with tenderness.

"Hey."

"Don't you get tired of the same book? I think by now you're an expert on fireflies."

Gabriel's mouth twitched in a tentative smile. He shrugged one shoulder. "It's the only audio we have, and really, I don't mind fireflies. But to be honest? I'm kind of over this book."

"Do you want me to read you another one? We have time before Papi calls us for breakfast."

"If you're not too busy."

"I'm not too busy," she replied, and headed to the bookcase. "Which one do you want me to read?"

"The one about pirates," he said, and it sounded like a question. There was so much hope in his voice.

Two summers ago, Maven had read the pirate book to him and the triplets every day. By the time school had started that year, she never wanted to even hear about pirates again. But . . . now, thinking back on the littles' laughter when she pretended to be the parrot, who was the narrator of the story, she smiled. That had been a good summer. It seemed so long ago.

Maven bit her lip so he wouldn't think she was making fun of him. "It's still your favorite, isn't it?"

"Argh!" he growled, making a hook with his arm,

and winking as if he had an eye patch.

She sat on the bed, and he plopped next to her, as together, they went over the book, taking turns to read, making different voices for all the characters.

"Now that I can read, I can tell how you were changing all the words," Gabriel said.

She smiled, her secret uncovered. "I just wanted to make the story better."

"You're good at it," Gabriel said.

"At what?"

"At being a sister," Gabriel said. "And making funny adventures for me and our cousins. You're good at so many things!"

If only all these things he mentioned had any value in the real world, meaning school. She had an obligation to end Gabriel's far-fetched ideas about her.

"Not really, Gabe," she said. "I let you down yesterday when you wanted to talk to me."

Now it was Gabriel's turn to roll his eyes. "But you're here now, Maven!"

She stared at his little face, marveled that someone who could laugh for half an hour straight about a silly knock-knock joke could be so wise.

"Where is my brother and what have you done with him?" she asked.

Gabriel's forehead wrinkled in confusion, but just a second. And then, without missing a beat, his eyes widened, and he tried not to smile. He put his hands straight ahead and said in a robotic voice, "Take me to your master."

Maven yelped, pretending to be scared, and jumped off the bed. "Who are you?"

Gabriel grabbed a flashlight from his nightstand and held it behind his back. He flicked the light on and off and made a buzzing sound and then exclaimed, "Argh!"

Maven laughed. "What are you supposed to be?"

"A pirate alien firefly!" he said, as he chased her around the room. Lucho joined them, always ready to have fun.

They ran in circles until Maven let him catch her. They collapsed on the floor and laid on their backs, staring at the glowing constellations on the ceiling.

"Why were you sad at school yesterday?" she asked.

Gabriel turned to her and said, "Rita and I had a

fight because we were doing a group project, and I kind of took over. We said some mean things to each other. But when I got home, I called her from Papi's phone, and I apologized. She said it was all cool."

In superspeed, Maven thought about how the last few weeks she'd tried to do everything for the robotics project herself. Being the leader didn't mean doing everything! If she and Dominic joined forces, then they could all do so much better, as a team.

To make matters worse, she'd put the distance between her and her friends.

She had never called Gemma or Sylvie after she missed them on Friday night. Was it wrong for them to click and become friends when that had been Maven's intention from the beginning? She had been super busy, but she couldn't expect her friends not to hang out together just because she chose to do something else. Besides, Maven hadn't been the best company lately. Not with her obsession about the competition. She'd believed she had to do everything perfectly to be cool and to fit in.

She just had to be herself, like she'd been with Gabriel.

"I'm sorry for making you sad," she said, and kissed the top of his head.

He smiled, but then there was a glint in his eye. "It's all good. But next time, you'll have to do my chores for a week!"

"Like I said, Gabi," she said, laughing. "You're wise beyond your years."

"Argh!"

Chapter Twenty

Her brother hadn't told her this in plain words, but after thinking and thinking about their conversation, Maven reached a conclusion: the secret to group-project success was teamwork.

She had known this, and yet, she had expected everyone to do what she said or else.

From this day on, she decided to channel her drive into being an empowering leader. There was a fine line, but she could do it.

First thing was talking to Dominic.

She waited for him at the exit to the playground. Every day, he and his group of friends headed to the four square to hog it from the rest of the school. They took turns playing and eating their sandwiches.

Maven had come prepared.

"Hey, Dominic," she said loud enough for him to hear her over the sound of so many students scrambling to get to the playground before anyone else.

He was so surprised that she was talking to him that he stopped in his tracks. "What?" he said, his eyes narrowed.

"As the class leaders for the robotics competition, we need to talk," she said.

"Oooh!" one of his cronies chanted. "Talk!" The way he said _talk_ made it seem like Maven had proposed holding hands or something. Her cheeks burned, but she held her ground.

"What are you worried about?" Sylvie chimed in. "Or are you scared of her?"

Maven hadn't explained to any of the girls what she had planned on doing, but she was grateful that Sylvie had come to her rescue again. Even when Maven had been so cold with her lately.

In the meantime, silence had fallen over the hallway. It was so heavy and electric at the same time that Mrs. Wagner poked her head out of the classroom to check that everything was okay. She saw the whole scene in front of her, but she must have guessed what Maven's plan was all along, because she just nodded once and went back into the classroom. She left the door open though, as if she wanted to hear every word.

"I think it's time we said everything out in the open for the sake of our class," she said. "I don't want our class to have the worst robot ever just because you and I don't get along."

Dominic looked at her for a couple of seconds. His blue eyes darted over his friends' faces, as if he were trying to ask for help on what to say. He swallowed his objections, and then nodded.

Maven exhaled the breath she was holding, and it was like someone had opened a window, judging by how many other people sighed in relief too.

"I don't want to miss lunch," he said.

She held up her lunch box and said, "Want some of mine? My mom always packs extra." When he hesitated, she added, "It's peanut butter and honey."

Dominic smiled and nodded. "Thanks!"

The rest of the crowd dissipated, with people heading to the cafeteria or the playground. Maven walked toward the kindergarten jungle gym. There were a couple of girls chatting inside one of the tunnels, Ariel selling her slime most likely, but it didn't matter. What Maven wanted to say wasn't a secret.

"Go ahead," Dominic said. "What do you want to say?"

Maven's heart started pounding all of a sudden. She didn't know why she was so nervous now. The worst part had been getting his attention.

"I just wanted to say you were right."

Dominic froze, the half-chewed bite of the PB-and-honey sandwich hanging in his mouth.

"Are you okay?" she asked, taking a step toward him in case he accidentally choked.

He swallowed and nodded. Putting a hand up as if to stop her, he said, "Did you say I . . . was right?"

She crossed her arms. "Yes. You were right when you said I didn't know anything about robotics."

There was a brief, heavy silence as Dominic seemed to consider these words.

"I wasn't expecting you'd ever say that, but, thanks, I guess."

The smug look on his face almost made Maven regret doing this. But she plunged forward with her plan. "I don't know much about robotics, and I realized you and I don't need to learn all about it for our class to succeed. Zahara and Claire know way more than anyone else in our class."

"But they don't want to be the leaders. I don't know about Claire, but Zahara just wants to read those books and be left alone," Dominic said.

"Exactly," Maven continued. "Which makes you and me the best project leaders. I've seen you direct the boys at four square. You know their strengths and weaknesses. Like I know most of the girls in our class. Instead of being divided, we need to join forces. We're one team after all."

"And how do we do that?" he asked. The smirk had fallen from his face.

He took the last bite of the sandwich and while he was occupied eating, she said, "You and I make a truce."

"A what?"

"We call for peace. For now. Not that we have to become friends or anything. Although we could, you know. But we stop sabotaging each other. Let's make sure the idea we all end up voting for is the best, the most original. Then we assign tasks to different groups, put everything together, and win the contest."

Dominic was quiet for a moment. Maven thought he'd say no and walk away.

But maybe he too was tired of fighting. Or he wanted to win more, and now they had a chance.

"Deal," he said, sticking out his hand for her to shake.

"Deal," she said, and shook his hand. Then she wiped the stickiness of honey off on her jeans. "Let's go tell the class we need to be united. Then we get to work."

Dominic looked shocked, like he too couldn't believe that things could be so simple. He gave her a nod and started walking away.

"One last thing," she said, and he turned back toward her as if her words had been a giant hand holding him back.

"What?"

"Open up the four square."

"Why should I do that?" he said, but his voice had a hint of laughter. "We got it first on the first day of school. It's a fifth-grade boy thing."

"It's a silly fifth-grade boy thing to exclude the girls. It will be way more fun if anyone can use it, like, Sylvie, for example."

"Do you think she's better than Gemma?"

It was a test, she could tell. Depending on what she replied, the whole conversation could turn into nothing.

"No one is better than anyone else," she said. "Like boys aren't better than girls, and vice versa. But sharing is the right thing to do."

He thought for a second and then nodded. "Okay."

He walked away and talked to the boys who'd gathered around him to hear the gossip he brought. Several of them looked in Maven's direction. She held their gazes, although the scaries were being particularly loud and annoying, their chattering voices like those of chipmunks.

But then Maven realized it wasn't the scaries. It was two fourth graders, Ariel and Faith, who'd been chatting in the tunnel and had witnessed the whole conversation.

"I'm going to ask," Ariel said. "What can they say? No?" She slid down the pole and took off toward the four square. The friend stood next to Maven and watched her. They couldn't hear what Ariel and Dominic said from this distance, but a couple of seconds later, the first girl had taken Logan's spot at the four square.

"Look at that!" Faith said.

Maven smiled bright like the sun. "Look at that."

Her plan had worked!

Chapter Twenty-One

Mrs. Wagner wasn't in the classroom, so Maven took the chance to apologize to her class. She stood on her desk chair and clapped her hands. This usually caught the triplets' attention. It didn't fail her now.

Everyone turned in her direction. Sylvie looked surprised, but she smiled.

Maven cleared her throat and said, "Hmm. Hey, I wanted to take a second to say I'm sorry for trying to take over the whole project."

"But you're the leader," Ben said. "You and Dominic."

"Right," Maven replied, and next to her Dominic nodded. She hadn't seen him step on Sylvie's desk chair. "We're the leaders, and our job should've been uniting the class, not getting into this boy-girl rivalry."

Dominic raised his hand, and Maven motioned at him to speak. "It was my fault too. What I said about girls not being good enough to be leaders was wrong." He swallowed, and Maven felt sympathy for him. She knew only too well how bitter it was to swallow one's pride.

"Claire's idea is the best of all, so I was proved wrong in all counts," he said.

Claire's cheeks were bright red with surprise at his words, and Maven sent Dominic a thumbs-up that he accepted with a nod of his head.

Who would've thought it would take so little to turn everyone's attitude? An apology goes a long way, and Maven was glad that she and Dominic had figured out how to work together.

The group turned to work on their proposal with gusto, and a few days later, it was time to decide on the one project that would represent the whole class.

After Claire had presented her idea of the pet walker, it was Sawyer's turn to defend his about a fish that glowed a different color if the temperature of a tank wasn't ideal.

"Isn't that a little too complicated for our class?" Zahara asked, echoing the question going through Maven's mind.

"My group did the research," Sawyer said. "The coding will be a little tricky, but Mrs. Wagner said a class did something similar two years ago and it worked."

Finally, Mrs. Wagner said, "Now let's count the votes."

Sylvie and Ben stood in front of a bowl full of pieces of paper with everyone's choices.

The atmosphere was crackling with anticipation, not because the final bell of the day would ring any minute now but because the whole class was fully invested in the outcome.

"And the winner is," Sylvie said. "Pet walker!"

Everyone exploded in cheers. Sawyer shrugged, but he shook hands with Claire and said, "Good job."

Maven and Dominic were bursting with pride that the class had all agreed on the best option, even if the idea had been a girl's.

Mrs. Wagner assigned the tasks for bringing the project from idea to robot: one group would write the report, another would code the software, and a third would build the prototype.

A group would make posters. Then two kids from the class would be chosen to present at the district fair.

The bell rang, and Mrs. Wagner waved goodbye. For the first time since she'd announced the contest, she seemed relieved.

"Good job bringing the class together, you two!" she said to Maven and Dominic as the rest of the class filed out. "I'm so proud of you!"

Maven caught Dominic's eye as he said, "Maven took the first step. I just followed along."

"Thank you" was all she managed to say. Even the scaries in her mind had gone silent.

"You're cool, Maven. Now I have to run, or I'll be late to football practice."

He dashed out to the sidewalk, and Maven followed, a smile on her face.

He'd said she was cool.

And she felt cool. Until she saw Gemma and Sylvie on the sidewalk whispering like they had a secret.

Chapter Twenty-Two

It wasn't the first time Maven had seen Gemma and Sylvie after the aquarium. During the couple of Girl Scout meetings they'd had, she had pretended nothing was the matter. That she'd gotten over her hurt feelings.

Maybe now she could just keep pretending that nothing had bothered her. Pretend that things were fine, and wait for . . .

For what exactly? For her temper to bubble until she said the wrong thing and ruined two friendships over words she didn't really mean?

No. Pretending things were perfect, like the whole school had pretended it was okay for the fifth-grade boys to hog the four square court, was just plain wrong. And she was done with all the drama. Even if there was a little when she told Gemma and Sylvie how she felt, at least everything would be out in the open and she'd be at peace.

Her dad's words rang in her mind, "The only way out is through."

Maven took a deep breath and headed toward them. Her little brother and Rita played tag by the flag-pole. Their joy at being together again was contagious.

"Hi," she said, and her voice was a little wobbly, just like her determination.

To make matters worse, at the sound of her voice, Sylvie and Gemma jumped.

"Hey!" they said as if they'd rehearsed it. They exchanged a guilty glance. The fact that they already communicated in silent looks bugged Maven, she had to admit.

"I'm sorry for the other day," Gemma said.

Maven hadn't expected an apology. "What?"

Sylvie cleared her throat. "Just that the other day at the aquarium. You got blamed because we were mis-behaving."

"And you didn't snitch on us," Gemma said.

"You also didn't get mad at us," Sylvie added.

Maven poked at the ground with the toe of her shoe and winced. "Actually . . . I was upset at you two." Her eyes filled with tears, but she continued. "And I was even more upset to see you were hanging out without me."

Gemma and Sylvie exchanged a mortified look.

Sylvie spoke up. "The day I invited you to the movies and you were busy, I was going to stay home, but I had Gemma's number. I didn't think you'd mind if we hung out together. I'm sorry that we kept hanging out without you."

It was true Sylvie had tried to include her in her plans, but Maven had been too busy. What was even worse, since Sylvie was the one new in the area and school, Maven should've been the one helping her adapt. She'd complained how Gemma always had soccer and didn't seem to make time for friends (aka Maven), and she'd done the same thing.

"I know . . ." she said. "I'm sorry. I've been obsessed with the robotics competition, and I didn't realize how I was blowing you off."

Gemma placed a hand on her shoulder. "It's okay, Maven. We hurt your feelings, and I'm sorry, too."

"I told Gemma how you handled the rift with the

boys and how hard you fought for Claire's idea. Your final vote gave her the victory."

"How do you know which one was my vote?" Maven searched Sylvie's eyes for the answer.

Sylvie shrugged. "I recognized your handwriting."

"The perfect cursive!" Gemma said.

The girls laughed.

Maven blushed. "I wrote all summer, you know. And when you practice something a lot, you get kind of good at it."

"What were you writing?" Sylvie asked. "Summer homework?"

Maven hesitated. But she remembered she wasn't going to pretend or hide anymore. She didn't need to. She didn't know a whole lot about Sylvie, but if her apology was an indication of something, it was that Sylvie was a good friend. And friends don't make fun of each other's interests and passions.

"No, not homework. Stories."

"Stories?"

Maven nodded. "This summer I organized a camp for my brother and our cousins. They're triplets. They have a lot of energy, and we were stuck at home. So I made this program to keep them—and me—entertained. We didn't have cool vacations like everyone else."

"You did what?" Sylvie asked. There was a curious glint in her eye.

"She organized a camp! She makes up the most amazing stories, and then she organizes these events around them! She creates adventures and then brings treats to match the theme. With Maven, you'll never be bored a day in your life." Gemma's chest puffed out with pride.

Maven was speechless.

"You mean you don't get bored when I'm around?" Maven asked.

Now Gemma was the one who looked confused. "What? Never! The only reason I could ever make it through the day was because I knew I had you by my side, Mave. I miss you so much!"

"You do?"

"Of course, silly! And not only that, but you have a gift for matching people with things and people they love."

"You're the coolest girl in the whole school," Sylvie said, and there was awe in her voice.

Maven bit her lip that was trembling.

"Do you forgive us?" Gemma asked.

Maven closed her eyes to savor this feeling. Not the validation that her friends' apology gave her, but the feeling of being loved and appreciated for who she was, quirks and all.

When she opened them again, Gemma and Sylvie looked like they were holding their breath.

"So?" they asked like a chorus. "Do you?"

"Of course!" she said, and flung her arms around them.

The next week, after Girl Scouts, where they learned first aid from Maven's mom, Vanessa and Maggie called Maven aside. Was she in trouble? She tried to shoo the thought away. She was done with the scaries, which always tried to yell the worst-case scenario and ended up getting her in trouble. Besides, she'd done nothing wrong.

"Don't look so worried," Maggie said, patting her shoulder. "It's nothing serious."

Maven's shoulders relaxed.

"Last week when you weren't here, Gemma and

Sylvie told me that they were the ones misbehaving at the aquarium and that you took the blame. Sorry I was so stern."

Maven glanced at her friends, who were too far to hear the conversation but who looked like they had tiny antennas pointing in her direction to read her every reaction.

"It's okay," she said.

"I know," Vanessa said, placing a hand on Maven's shoulder. "You're a great friend and leader, Maven. I just wanted to let you know."

"You're a wonderful example of everything a Girl Scout is supposed to be. Keep on being so awesome."

She couldn't help it now. She was grinning from ear to ear.

It was wonderful when her friends had apologized and had accepted her apology in return. And it was great to learn from grown-ups who weren't afraid to show they weren't perfect and acknowledged it. It made it easier to believe that she didn't have to be perfect to be loved and accepted.

It was a cool feeling. One that Maven hoped would stay.

Chapter Twenty-Three

During the next three weeks, Maven and Dominic led the class as a true team to gather the materials and then dive into the task of building their robot, the pet walker. True to herself though, a couple of nights before the class tested the prototype, Maven tried it at home with Lucho. It worked like a charm, and Lucho loved the extra treats his grateful human gifted him.

Maven was confident her class would win.

How could they not?

Although she still worked hard, Maven remembered to spend time with the people who meant the most to her. She even planned a brand-new adventure for Gabriel and the triplets. The littles declared that the fairy fair in Autumn Cove was the best one yet. But perhaps it was the extra sugary pumpkin soda that had made them so happy and hyper.

Maven still felt bubbly when, a few days before the competition, Claire (who was the driver, the one person in charge of controlling the robot so her pet hamsters, Fluffy and Cheese, wouldn't be so nervous) successfully had the robot navigate the track one of the groups had built.

The whole class cheered, victorious.

"It's wonderful!" Mrs. Wagner said. "I'm so proud of you!" She praised the whole class but looked longer at Maven and Dominic.

Maven felt her chest was about to explode with pride. All the stress and hard work had been worth it! She was so happy that she invited Gemma and Sylvie to the movies to celebrate.

But the day of the competition, she was still nervous. She wasn't the only one with jitters though.

Dominic tried not to show it, but by now, Maven knew him well enough to recognize the signs. His face was so pale his freckles popped. They were adorable. Not that Maven would ever confess this. But she wasn't above giving him a compliment he deserved.

"You look really good in your suit," she said. She moved her weight from one foot to the next. Her patent shoes were tighter than she had expected when she put them on to look her best for the robotics competition.

Dominic didn't quite smile, but the corners of his mouth tugged up. "You look nice too."

She beamed at him. The silver dress that Tía had gifted her for taking care of the triplets all summer was a little itchy, to be honest, but just a little. It made her feel like the most fashionable robot ever.

The floor of the convention center, where the competition was taking place, teemed with kids from all the schools of the district. Maven wished Gemma were here, but her school was part of another district. It didn't matter though. Maven was paying attention to every detail to tell her friend when they got together in the evening.

Maven had planned something special for Gemma and Sylvie.

"Do you think we have a shot?" Dominic asked, tugging at the collar of his dress shirt.

"Of course," she said sincerely, even though the

competition was tough.

The other fifth grade class from their school had turned in a drone that had a mini water spray. Cameron Lund said the whole class had helped, but Tatum Stephenson, who was this week's four square champion, had told Sylvie, who told Maven, that Cameron hadn't let anyone else work on the project. Rumor said his brother, who was *almost* an engineer, had done the whole thing.

Still, Maven didn't have time to worry about the other teams. Her team needed her—and Dominic—to keep them organized.

While Maven answered an administrator's questions about their presentation, Claire successfully showed off their robot all around the perimeter of their showcase area.

The administrator walked away, and Maven caught Dominic's eye. He stepped up next to her and said, "We had a mishap with the hamsters' food, but Zahara is on it."

"Everything under control?" she asked, trying to look over her shoulder. A group of kids from another school were blocking her vision though.

"Everything's under control," Dominic assured her.

"And the hamsters?"

"Sawyer's watching them." Dominic smiled mischievously. "He's so in love with them that he might not give them back to Claire!"

"We'll have to watch him carefully, then," Maven said.

A few feet away from them, Mimi was switching the hamster in the pet walker while Sawyer made sure she placed the harness on correctly . . .

"Is that Fluffy or Cheese?" Maven asked.

Dominic shrugged. "I can never tell."

They were laughing when Mrs. Callahan walked up to them. "I see everything worked out after all," she said.

Maven exhaled, the scaries a thing of the past. "It did. Thanks for all your help."

Mrs. Callahan nodded, satisfied. Then she turned toward Dominic. "Looks like the girls on the team knew about robotics after all, right?"

Maven stifled a giggle when Dominic blushed.

"We were lucky they did," he said.

A warm feeling spread in Maven. "We were lucky we all make a great team," she said.

Mrs. Callahan snapped her fingers. "That's the best kind of luck of all: knowing how to work together. Congratulations."

She walked away while Maven and Dominic beamed with pride.

After the superintendent and the committee had walked all over the floor looking at each project, clipboard in hand, it was finally time to announce the winning class.

Maven hadn't been worried, but now the palms of her hands prickled with nerves. Dominic's face was pinched too.

"Ladies and gentlemen," the superintendent announced.

A hush went over the room. Mrs. Wagner's fifth grade class huddled together to hear the results.

"First of all, we're so impressed with everyone's efforts. Congratulations! We love to see your ingenuity and teamwork."

Some people from other schools snickered. It was obvious other classes had struggled with this project.

But Maven knew her class had given its all. Once they'd put their differences aside.

"The winner is . . ."

She looked at Dominic, whose skin had turned a shade of green that didn't look like good news. Maven hesitated for a second, but then she grabbed his hand and said, "Breathe, Nic. You're going to be okay."

"It's the nerves," he said.

"I call them the scaries," said Maven.

He smiled, looking relieved that someone understood what he was feeling and didn't make fun of him.

Together they turned ahead to listen to the results, but Maven didn't let go of his hand, and he didn't shake her off. People would gossip, but she did it in the spirit of being a good leader and team member.

"The winner is Autumn Ridge Elementary and their Litter Picker!"

All around them, cheers exploded. But Maven still heard Logan's disappointed, "No! It's not fair!"

That's exactly how she felt.

The warmth and giddiness she had felt seconds ago vanished, and tears burned her eyes. She looked down at her shoes, embarrassed her team hadn't won first place. But when she looked up, she saw her class-mates all united, congratulating the winners and each other. Zahara and Claire were hugging, their faces a mixture of sadness and . . . pride. Sawyer was pet-ting both hamsters in his arms while Mimi fed them carrots.

Even the hamsters had done their best, and they deserved a treat.

"Oh well," Dominic said. "At least it's obvious that the Litter Picker was planned and made by kids. Not like the drone."

His frown made him look so sad. Maven's eyes filled with tears again, this time with sympathy.

But there was no time or room for tears. The whole of Mrs. Wagner's class huddled in a group hug around their teacher and the project leaders—Maven and Dominic.

"I'm so impressed with all of you!" their teacher said, her arms stretched out as if she wanted to em-brace them all. "This was my favorite project yet!"

"But we didn't win!" said Christopher.

"What do you mean?" asked Mrs. Wagner. "Look at our class! I think we got the best prize of all!" She looked at Maven and Dominic as she said this and then turned to see the whole class working and having fun together, boys and girls.

When the disassembling committee was packing up the pet walker, Mrs. Wagner said, "Great job, Maven! I'm really proud of you."

"Thank you," she said, giddy with relief that this was all done but also proud that true to her pledge, she had stuck with it even when things got tough. Especially then.

"Do you think you'll join the robotics club next year at the middle school?"

Maven flinched. "Probably not. Robotics is definitely *not* my thing." She wasn't ashamed of saying this aloud.

"But there are other things that you learn at robotics club: like leadership, teamwork, and goal setting. Although I'm sure you didn't just learn these traits during the robotics project."

Maven shook her head and laughed. "No, I learned by being a Girl Scout!"

Mrs. Wagner gave her a huge smile. "Yes, I knew it the moment you volunteered. I was a Girl Scout too!"

Then she asked, "I'm curious. . . . What's one of your passions, then?"

"Storytelling," she said, aware of Dominic's gaze on her. Her cheeks warmed, but she added, "I love to write and make up fun adventures for little kids."

"Then you're going to love our next unit on fairy tales."

Maven felt like she was glowing. She'd grown these past few weeks, but she was sure looking forward to diving into something that was challenging and that she absolutely loved.

Later, when Maven was stepping off the bus, Dominic said, "Bye, Mave."

"Bye, Nic."

"Beat you tomorrow at four square—I mean, see you tomorrow at school."

"Sure!" She had tried to answer all casual, but she was delighted. Being cool was being comfortable being yourself and loving what you love.

And it was even cooler to know that her friends, old and new, liked her for what and who she really was.

Chapter Twenty-Four

The sun was sinking quickly under the horizon, and Maven got excited.

She'd timed this adventure precisely. In two minutes, her best friends were going to get the show of their lives. But if they didn't hurry, they were going to miss it.

"Come on, slowpokes!"

Behind her, Gemma and Sylvie were carrying a giant picnic basket. "Coming!"

They made it to the top of Fairy Meadow just in time. The trees were gilded in every shade of gold and rust. Maven may have planned the outing, but Mother Nature had given her a hand. The mist from the nearby creek gave the scene the touch of magic

Maven could only dream about.

Finally at the top, they laid-out a checkered table-cloth and little sandwiches and drinks. Gemma's EpiPen poked from the basket. There were no bees this time in the season, but just in case, you never know. . . .

Gemma stretched her long legs, all bruised and banged up from soccer. Sylvie was massaging her feet. They'd had practice that day and they were tired, but they wouldn't have missed this picnic with Maven for the world.

"What do you think?" Maven asked.

"It's incredible," said Sylvie.

"Superb. I'm impressed that you could pull strings and manage to get the clouds to look exactly like spa-ghetti and meatballs just for us."

Gemma was joking, of course. Although the clouds were all swirly and reddish in the last light of the day. Maven told them a story she'd prepared just for her friends. She hadn't made it up, but she found it in one of the old fairy tale books her dad had borrowed from the library for her.

"Here," she said, handing her friends a bound book

she'd made with recycled paper and pressed flowers. "I wrote the story here if you want to read it on your own another day."

"You're amazing," said Sylvie.

"We all are," said Maven, trying to be modest but loving that her friends thought she was cool even with her quirks.

"We start indoor soccer in a couple of weeks," said Gemma. "You should join us."

Maven shrugged. "You know I like to watch you play, but I don't play myself."

"It's cool," said Gemma. "We need a team manager."

"I don't know the rules of soccer."

Sylvie scoffed. "I'm pretty sure learning them will be easier than learning how to make robots, Mave! Besides, it's not like you don't already have a bunch of books about it at your house already. I saw them when I arrived."

Maven shrugged. "I wanted to learn the lingo to catch up with you two."

"Come on," said Gemma. "It will be fun and we'll get to spend more time together."

She looked at Maven with those puppy eyes Maven couldn't resist. "Will you say yes? Your mom said she was okay with it if you said yes."

Maven pretended to roll her eyes, but she was delighted that her friends had thought of including her this way.

"I'll see," she said. If their practices weren't on the nights she reserved for storytelling with Gabi and the triplets, it could work. She actually had been considering joining the robotics club next year at the middle school. But that was a year away. The opportunity to spend more time with her friends *was* priceless. She would say yes.

"Talking about learning a new lingo, did you hear me practicing my dogginese with Lucho? They don't teach that in books," said Gemma.

"You have been practicing your what?" asked Sylvie.

"Her dog talk," Maven said, bursting into laughter.

Gemma shrugged one shoulder. She had a glint in her eyes. "Don't you remember? Our Girl Scout troop is going to volunteer at the animal shelter."

She started barking.

In the distance, a dog howled in response.

The three girls were rolling on the ground laughing.

Maven wasn't sure she'd ever perfect her dog talk like Gemma, but maybe her extreme organizational skills would come in handy. Again.

There was only one way to know.

Eric Hason

Yamile Saied Méndez is the author of many books for young readers and adults, including *Furia*, a Reese's YA Book Club selection and the 2021 inaugural Pura Belpré Young Adult Author Award winner, *Where Are You From?*, *Shaking Up the House*, and the Horse Country series, among others. She was born and raised in Rosario, Argentina, but has lived most of her life in a lovely valley surrounded by mountains in Utah. She's a graduate of Voices of Our Nations (VONA) and the Vermont College of Fine Arts MFA writing for children and young adults program and a founding member of Las Musas, a marketing collective of Latine writers. Visit her at yamilesmendez.com.